Throne of Threats

~A Court of Mystery Novel~

Book Five

Sarah E. Burr

This book is a work of fiction. Any similarity between the characters and situations within its pages and places or persons, living or dead, is unintentional and coincidental.

Copyright © 2018 by Sarah Burr

All rights reserved. This book or any portion thereof may not be reproduced or used in any manner whatsoever without the express written permission of the publisher except for the use of brief quotations in a book review.

First Printing, 2018
This edition, 2025

www.saraheburr.com

Other books by Sarah E. Burr

The Court of Mystery series

The Ducal Detective
A Feast Most Foul
A Voyage of Vengeance
A Summit in Shadow
Throne of Threats
Paradise Plagued
Burdened Bloodline
Sovereign Sieged
Crown of Chaos
Harrowed Heir
Ravaged Reign
Innocence Imprisoned
Ardent Ascension
Eternal Empire

More Cozy Mysteries by Sarah

Trending Topic Mysteries
Glenmyre Whim Mysteries
Book Blogger Mysteries

www.saraheburr.com

A brief history…

Centuries ago, the corrupt and powerful priests of the Ancient Faith lorded over the continent. Poverty and sickness ravaged the world, forcing a faction of rebels to rise up and overthrow these tyrants preaching in the name of silent gods. The leaders of this movement, known in the annals of history as the Rebirth, proclaimed the realm would no longer answer to nameless demons and gods, but to the virtues of bravery, humility, kindness, and intelligence. Under these Virtues, the world would once again flourish. Sealing their pact, these newly anointed leaders drank the dew of the fabled kingsleaf flower, ensuring their offspring would be marked as the divine protectors of this new era with their royal eyes.

Welcome to the Realm of Virtues.

The
Realm
of
Virtues
The
Brave Sea
Lysandeir
Cetachi
Pettraud
Kwatalar
Mensina
Crepsta
Saphire
The
Sea of
Humility
Zaltor
The
Sea of
Intelligence
Beautraud
Hestes
Tandora
Savant
The
Kind Sea
Isla
Delacqua

Chapter One

"Do you think we're making a mistake?"

The glint in Perry's lavender eyes revealed he was suppressing a wry smile. "What, by getting married?"

Jax tossed her arms up in feigned exasperation before collapsing into a fit of giggles. "Of course not. By choosing to get married at sunset. Won't the lighting be off?" She turned around to survey the grand room, sunlight seeping in through the glass ceiling, bathing the stone floor in gold. Picturing it lined with dark wood pews and bouquets of orchids and irises, she couldn't help but smile.

Perry rested a hand on her shoulder, pulling her close to his chiseled chest. "Why don't we take a stroll through here this evening and see for ourselves?"

"Just the two of us?" Jax raised her amethyst eyes, meeting his intense stare.

"Just us," he said, sealing the promise with a kiss on her forehead. "But for now, why don't we tell these lovely ladies where you'd like your guests to sit." Perry motioned to the eight assembled women who were staring at them both with envy.

For a moment, Jax had forgotten her army of wedding planners were there. Perry tended to have that effect on her. Trying to distract the group from her blushing cheeks, she cleared her throat. "I think it makes sense to sit Tandora and Beautraud on Perry's side of the aisle." She looked at her fiancé to clarify. "Since your father recently visited both duchies, it might be nice to have their representation on the Pettraudian side."

Perry nodded in agreement, happy to let her do the heavy lifting when it came to figuring out where to put each duchy's delegation.

"And I think I'll give you Crepsta as well," Jax said with a slight scowl. "The Duke might see it as a bit of a slight. No offense, but I just can't find it in my heart to have his nation in my pews." Shuddering, the ghost of betrayal tapped her shoulder. While Duke Crepsta had not been directly involved with the deaths of her beloved parents nearly two years ago, the role his family had played in the murderous plot still overshadowed their once strong relationship.

"I think that's a splendid idea," Perry whispered, wrapping his arm around her slender waist. "Father and the Duke recently participated in some type of hunting trip together, so I'm sure they won't see any offense in it at all."

"Wonderful." Jax clasped her hands, pleased that everything seemed to be falling into place. "Then we'll put the other leaders on my side."

"What about the guests not with a royal delegation, Your Grace?" one of the women spoke up, her tone laden with reverence.

Jax thought fondly of the friends she would be hosting in just a few hours' time. She had selectively invited some of her closest acquaintances, asking them to arrive a few days earlier than the realm's leaders she was required to invite out of respect. "I think they'll know which side to sit on." She grinned at Perry, knowing he, too, was looking forward to the arrival of some of his close friends from Pettraud, none of whom Jax had never met.

The wedding planners looked cautiously at each other, and she wondered if they were secretly planning to make assignments anyways. After all, they were tasked with making sure every detail of her wedding day was perfect.

The creaking of a side door rang throughout the chapel. "Your Grace?" Uma's delicate voice emerged from the shadows before her petite figure did. "It appears a few of your guests have just arrived. Shall I show them to their rooms, or would you like to greet them personally?"

Jax waved the throng of wedding planners back to work, crossing the length of the room to reach Uma's side. "I'll greet them in person, of course. Anything to be free of these asinine questions." She examined the bashful face of her lady-in-waiting. "I thought *you* were going to be the one in charge of planning this whole celebration?" she teased.

Uma smoothed back her mousey brunette hair, her lovely brown eyes resting directly on the Duchess. "Even though I've been by your side for far too long, I'm not a mind reader. You do need to tell those women a few details."

Jax opened her mouth to spout a snappy retort, but Uma held up a hand to silence her. "This is the last thing I need your opinion on. I may be more well-versed with the political goings on of the realm than I was a few months ago, but I figured you are the best one to determine who sits where."

Jax had to give Uma credit for knowing her strengths. The young woman, who had come into Jax's life as her lady's maid over a decade ago, was now one of her closest friends and her trusted lady-in-waiting. Yet, she was still learning the ropes of the position normally held by a noblewoman. Uma was the first common-born person in the Realm of Virtues to be appointed to such a prestigious role, as Jax had done away with tradition and bestowed the position to someone who truly deserved it. It was one of the radical changes that had come about in the realm after a particularly tumultuous peace summit last winter.

Perry sauntered up to Uma. "Any of these early arrivals here to see me?" he asked with boyish glee.

"Unfortunately, your horde has not yet arrived," she replied with wry bemusement.

He laughed at the remark, then addressed Jax. "All right, then. I'll let you catch up with your friends before I crash the party, my dear. I'll be out in the gardens with my easel." With a quick kiss, he dismissed himself, and Jax watched him amble away, appreciating the sight.

"How are you feeling?" Uma asked for what felt like the hundredth time that day.

"The same as I felt twenty minutes ago when you deposited me here with these women."

Uma rolled her eyes, used to the flippant way her Duchess addressed her innermost feelings. "You will let me know if it all becomes too much, won't you?"

Sensing her friend's true concern, Jax squeezed her arm. "I won't say I don't feel my parents' absence, but I truly am looking forward to the festivities, dear one." She prayed to the Virtues that her parents, the late Duke and Duchess of Saphire, were watching down on her so that she could share her special day with them.

Satisfied, Uma took her by the arm and led her down a long hallway, through which they weaved their way to the castle entrance. "Lady Carriena has arrived with a few others in tow."

Jax clasped her hands in delight. It had been nearly a year since she'd last seen her friend, the Crown Princess of Isla DeLacqua, and she was eager to catch up with her. "Wonderful! I'm so glad she was able to get here before all the boring people flood our halls."

"Boring people? I hope you don't mean me?" A smooth voice chuckled from behind a pillar.

"Darian? Goodness, you gave me a fright!" Jax laughed breathlessly before scooping up the strapping young man in a fierce hug. "When did you get in?" she asked, shooting a questioning look to a red-faced Uma.

"Don't blame poor Uma for not telling you. Annette and I were planning to surprise you at dinner this evening. Your aunt told me not to go traipsing about the castle because I'd no doubt run into you." Darian, the newly crowned Duke of Cetachi, ran a calloused hand through his wavy brown hair. "And I've done just that. Don't ever tell her I said this, but that woman is rarely wrong."

Jax smiled, thinking how much her aunt would enjoy hearing just that. "Well, I'm so glad you made it here early. How was the journey?" Cetachi was one of the northernmost territories in the realm and a land of mystery to her. Before Darian's ascension to the throne, Cetachi had been a lawless place with tribes adrift all over the region. Over the past six months or so, Darian had been working to unite his people under one banner.

With a playful shrug, he beamed. "It was uneventful. A nice

relief from my day-to-day life."

For the first time, she noticed how incredibly tired her friend looked. "I've heard you've been making good progress these past few months." Her questioning eyes sought confirmation.

"Yes, progress has been made. I'm still struggling with a few coastal hordes of wild men that seem intent on making life unpleasant for my people." Darian paused for a moment, his common-born brown eyes seeming to be hundreds of miles away. "Annette has arranged for some military assistance from Mensina, but I'm hopeful that it won't be needed. There's a nasty fever ripping through the wilds, and I've offered medicine in exchange for their cooperation."

This news surprised Jax in more ways than she cared to admit. "Mensina? Why wouldn't you come to us for aid?" Mensina lay to the east, ruled by her grandfather, from whom she had been estranged until recent years.

"We didn't want to bother you, dear, or sour your wedding preparations by sending away troops."

His earnest expression revealed his words to be the truth, but Jax couldn't help feeling a slight sting. After all, her duchy was the strongest, the largest, and by far the most influential throughout the Realm of Virtues. An upstart nation like Cetachi should have reached out to her for help. "I appreciate your concern, but personal feelings aside, you may need the strength of Saphire to see this matter through. I ask in the future, dear Darian, that you always remember Saphire is your greatest ally." She hoped she didn't sound too reprimanding, but it was imperative that he understand her power within the realm.

He gave her a graceful bow. "Forgive me, Jax. I am still new to this messy arena, and I fear sometimes Annette's love for you clouds her judgment. Saphire has nothing but Cetachi's deepest respect."

Jax commended him for admitting his mistake, as few people ever had the courage to do so. It represented yet another one of the admirable traits that made him such a good leader for his people. Regardless, she found Annette's decision concerning. Was it some secret ploy to empower Mensina as the realm's new savior? She pushed the dark thoughts out of her head for the moment, chastising herself for being so quick to mistrust her aunt's intentions. "All is forgiven. Now, when will I be able to call you 'Dear Uncle'?" she asked with a teasing grin.

Darian's pale skin flushed as he stumbled to find his words. It was no secret that Annette and the new Duke had grown incredibly fond of one another over the past few months. Annette had been serving as Darian's royal advisor in Cetachi, helping him navigate the political waters of the realm. "I'm hopeful it will be soon. Your grandfather, though, might have other plans in mind."

Jax couldn't contain a snort. "I'm sure he does. Don't be offended by it, though. My guess is that he's waiting for my wedding to wrap up so he can shine the spotlight on Mensina's daughter." Even though Duke Mensina loved and respected his granddaughter, he still had a duchy of his own to run.

"I hope you're right. I'm worried he's found a better match for Annette."

"My aunt would never allow it. Her heart lies with you," Jax said, her words ringing with heartfelt sincerity.

Darian gave her an enthusiastic grin before clearing his throat. "Well, if you wouldn't mind, pretend you haven't seen me, Duchess. My royal advisor doesn't need to know about this little run in."

Chuckling, she agreed. "I'll see you during our long-awaited reunion at dinner."

With a nod of farewell to Uma, Darian Fangard sauntered down the hall.

Jax had nearly forgotten the presence of her lady-in-waiting, who'd been practically invisible during their conversation. "You're far too good at being a fly on the wall, dear one."

Uma smiled, swelling with pride at the observation. "Jaquobie says it is a vital skill to maintain if I'm to serve you well, Duchess."

"Of course he would say that." Jax couldn't resist a theatrical eye roll at the advice her High Courtier had given Uma. As her highest ranking royal advisor, he would value anyone who had the ability to obtain information without being detected.

"Shall we?" Uma motioned down the hall.

"Only if you promise not to keep visitors within my castle walls a secret," Jax said lightly, not wanting to rebuke her friend too severely. "I know it might seem all fun and games, especially with Annette being my aunt, but a sovereign can never be too careful."

Uma's face paled. "Goodness, Jax, I didn't even think of it that way." She shook her head as her shoulders sagged. "Doesn't it wear you down, having to think in such dark terms all the time?"

"Seems like second nature to me now," Jax mused. She had experienced more betrayal and deceit than she'd ever expected and had learned her lesson when it came to blindly putting her trust in people. "Come now, we both know Lady Carriena does not like to be kept waiting, especially when making an entrance."

Chapter Two

The playful chatter in the entryway floated up the remaining length of the hall, and a smile grew steadily wider on Jax's face. It was impossible to mistake Carriena's vibrant voice as it drowned out those of her traveling companions.

Walking past the archway and into a pool of light that streamed in through the open doors, Jax felt arms wrap around her before her eyes had time to adjust.

"Jacqueline!" Carriena shrieked, forgetting all sense of decorum. "You look beautiful, darling. Oh, it's been too long." Her words rapidly tumbled out of her mouth.

Jax pulled back from the strong grip to assess her friend properly. Carriena's short blond hair had been bleached nearly white by the sun, no doubt from spending her days on the beaches of Isla DeLacqua, the realm's only island nation. Her blue traveling gown was simple, but made from the finest materials gold could buy, accenting her pale lavender eyes perfectly. "You look lovely as well, dearest. It appears you've been able to escape the confines of your father's court and enjoy the sun."

Carriena nodded, delicately fanning herself. "It has been unseasonably warm this spring, especially in the isles. I'm glad you're getting married now, because we'll all be sweltering in our dresses in a few weeks' time."

Jax caught a glimpse of two more figures entering the hall and her eyes brightened even more. "Oh, I am so glad you two were able to arrive early."

Before speaking, Charles Montivarius dropped to one knee in a deep bow. "We were delighted that Lady Carriena was able to make travel arrangements for us all."

From his side, his younger sister curtsied. "Yes, it was easy enough for Charles, as he is still doing his residency under Duke DeLacqua's court physician. Lady Carriena went above and beyond, though, coming to Hestes to collect me before heading north." Lady Giovanna gave her traveling companion a grateful smile. "I would have offered to meet them at the Tandora port, but I had to contend with the final performance of Father's latest production."

Charles and Giovanna were the offspring of the renowned playwright, Michelangelo Montivarius. While Charles's calling had led him to become a court physician, Giovanna was a gifted actress and often the star of her father's shows.

Carriena leaned in and whispered to Jax in a devilish tone, "I really just wanted the chance to collect a barrel of Hestes's spring wine."

Suppressing the urge to snort, Jax reached out a hand and gave Giovanna's arm a fond squeeze. "I'm so glad the timing worked out. It's been too long since I've seen you all. Your father will join us for the ceremony, yes?"

Charles nodded, running a hand over his close-cut ashen hair. "Indeed. I imagine he'll be looking for inspiration for his next production while he's here."

Jax blushed, knowing her exploits had been the subject of one of Michelangelo's most successful plays to date. "Well, considering he's here for a simple wedding, I doubt he'll have much drama to observe."

"Simple wedding? I hope not," Carriena said, feigning shock before greeting Uma with a hug. "I was promised a grand affair, was I not?"

Uma chuckled at the royal's candidness. "Jax has been trying to convince herself for weeks that all this isn't a big deal. You know how she gets."

Carriena's lavender eyes, the mark of a ducal bloodline, narrowed, her attention honing in on Jax. "You're allowed to celebrate, you know that, right? This is a monumental occasion. You don't get married every day."

Waving a hand aside, the Duchess ushered her guests to follow her into the castle. "I know. It just helps calm my nerves, that's all."

"Nerves? Whatever are you nervous about?" Giovanna asked, her button nose wrinkling in confusion.

Jax looked at her companions, unease written all over her face. "I don't know. I just feel like I'm too happy. I can't rid myself of the feeling that something is about to burst my bubble."

Charles folded his sinewy arms across his chest. "Have you been sleeping well of late?" His frayed physician robes swished across the stone floor as they walked, a reminder of his expertise.

Nodding, Jax waited while two of the palace guards pushed open the large doors to the banquet hall. "Again, I'm sure it's just nerves. It's been a while since Saphire has hosted so many delegations from around the realm." Due to the circumstances surrounding her hasty coronation, many of the other leaders had not been able to attend on such short notice.

"I'm sure Uma is doing everything in her power to make it all seem effortless," Carriena commented, her eyes flickering to the lady-in-waiting.

Something in Carriena's gaze unsettled Jax. It almost looked as though she were giving Uma some kind of warning.

Unfazed, Uma simply smiled. "The only thing I'm worried about is Jax getting wedding cake all over her dress. Everything else is already arranged and taken care of."

The reference to Jax's love of sweets sent the group into giggles as they cascaded through the doorway into the grand dining room.

"All right, I shall leave you all to catch up. I have a few items to attend to. Please do not hesitate to reach out to me directly if there are any questions or concerns about your rooms," Uma said before gracefully bowing out of the small reunion.

"She seems to be taking her job seriously," Carriena muttered under her breath as Uma glided away, loud enough for Jax to hear.

The Duchess frowned at the not-so-subtle tone. "Whatever is

that supposed to mean? Why wouldn't she?"

"Well," Carriena shrugged, "it's just I wasn't expecting her to be so good at her role, in all honesty."

Charles and Giovanna exchanged timid looks with one another, clearly uncomfortable with the topic Carriena had broached.

Jax's brow furrowed. "I hope you're not suggesting Uma incapable of the position simply because of her common-born roots."

Carriena paused, looking around as if gauging the reactions of the audience gathered around her. "Well, I mean, it's not as if there's ever been a common-born lady-in-waiting before, Jax. Of course, I'm surprised."

Folding her arms, the Duchess looked at her friend with muted disgust. "I would have thought you of all people would be supportive of my decision."

Carriena's eyes narrowed at the heat in Jax's words. "Why? Because I know Uma personally? Yes, she's been your shadow since the Academy, but I never saw her as more than a lady's maid. I was surprised as anyone by your announcement naming her your lady-in-waiting. I mean, it shook the very foundations that the realm was built upon. Not to mention we now have a common-born Duke."

Since the Rebirth, a time long ago when the corrupt overlords of the land were deposed and the Realm of Virtues was founded, the duchies had been ruled by royal blood, descended from those first anointed when the realm was established. Darian Fangard, with the support of Jax and her allies, was the first common-born man to rise to the station of Duke, becoming the leader of Cetachi. At the time of this historic decision, Jax had also announced that Uma would be her lady-in-waiting, hoping to signal change across the duchies that commoners could rise to positions normally reserved for those from noble houses. It was clear from Carriena's reaction that the decision had not been received as warmly as Jax would have liked. But she asked the more important question that this was all leading to. "Does your father feel the same as you?"

Carriena waved a hand. "I'm not sure he even fully understands what you've done. He actually laughed at a petition made by one of our common folk to become a Courtier."

Jax thanked the Virtues Uma was not around to hear this

conversation. "Well then, I shall make it a point to talk with him when he arrives for the ceremony. Both you and he might benefit from speaking with Duke Cetachi."

"It sounds so odd to hear that title." Charles jumped into the conversation, looking as if he desperately wanted to change the subject. "After growing up hearing stories of the wild north, to now see it civilized is truly amazing."

"Yes, and Darian Fangard sounds like a fascinating young man. Father so badly wants to meet him," Giovanna chimed in. "I think he'd make for a dashing protagonist in a new drama."

Jax gave the siblings a gracious smile. "I shall make the introduction personally, then. I do think you'll enjoy his company," she said, with a pointed look at Carriena. "Until then, may I interest any of you in afternoon tea?" Her words heralded the arrival of the dining hall staff pushing golden carts glittering with sweets and snacks.

"Perhaps I sounded cross because I haven't eaten in hours," a chastened Carriena conceded, her expression a silent plea for forgiveness.

Jax wrapped an arm around her friend's slender shoulders. "A cherry tart can cure anything." She laughed as she popped one of the fruity pastries into her mouth.

The remainder of the hour was free of tension, each of the four friends taking turns bringing everyone up to speed on the goings on in their lives.

Charles was just finishing a particularly outrageous tale about having to treat an entire delegation from Savant for wine poisoning when Perry entered the room.

Once hugs and greetings were exchanged, Perry sank into the chair next to Jax.

"Any pre-wedding jitters, Lord Pettraud?" Carriena asked with a teasing smile.

"Just that I can't believe it's finally happening. It seems like I've been waiting my whole life to marry this beauty," he said, squeezing Jax's hand with a reverent tenderness.

Giovanna looked completely smitten by the remark. "How romantic. I still cannot believe we were aboard the ship when you proposed," she said with a sigh, her words bringing them all back to the incredible sea voyage.

"What's hard to believe is that it took even that long for Perry to pop the question," Carriena quipped, grabbing another chocolate biscuit to stuff in her mouth.

Perry held up his hands in surrender. "How many times do I have to apologize for being slow on the uptake?" he joked.

Jax noticed his palms were smudged with blue and green paint. "How is your latest project coming along?" she asked, picturing him hard at work at his easel in the blossoming palace gardens.

He wagged a finger in answer. "You know it's a surprise. You'll just have to wait and see, Duchess."

Jax, never fond of waiting, rolled her eyes in response.

"I was expecting to be surrounded by strapping young men during this celebration, Perry." Carriena sat up in her chair and looked around the massive hall, empty save for their little gathering. "Jax promised me handsome faces to fawn over. Where are all your friends?"

Running a hand through his dark, curly hair, Perry blushed. "Well, I thought they'd be here by now, but I guess my friends aren't as keen to see me as you all were."

Even though he hadn't shared much about his guest list, Jax had risked a quick peek at the invitations before Uma had sent them out. It looked like Perry had invited a handful of Pettraudian lords, but it surprised Jax that none of them were his brothers. Perry was the youngest of seven sons, but since he hardly ever spoke about them, anyone would think he had no siblings. Only recently had Perry's relationship with his father improved, and that was due mostly to Perry saving his father from a maniacal killer last winter.

"Tell us about your friends," Carriena prodded. "I need to know who best to set my sights on."

Jax smiled inwardly, thanking her brazen friend for being the one to drag these details out of Perry. As much as Jax wanted to pry, she also didn't want to risk hounding him if he wasn't entirely comfortable sharing his former life in Pettraud.

Perry's crossed arms reflected his unease with the topic. "I'm not sure there's much to tell. I was introduced to the Viscounts through my father. I suppose I've known Edmund and Skander the longest. We were tutored together."

"Fascinating," Carriena drawled, rolling her eyes at Perry's unenthusiastic descriptions.

Jax searched her memory for their official titles. "Edmund is the Earl of Windale and Skander is the Baron of Eveluce?"

"Are those provinces in Pettraud?" Charles inquired. "I haven't been there in years."

Taking a long sip of now-lukewarm tea, Perry nodded in response to both questions. "Yes. I think you all will get along smashingly."

"Who are these Viscounts?" Giovanna asked.

"Bran and Emyr are the sons of Marquess Carwyn. He's one of the richest noblemen in Pettraud and a staunch friend of my father's. Our friendship was formed more out of necessity than desire." A slight frown danced across Perry's angular features. "Not that they aren't decent blokes. In fact, I think Carriena will find Emyr particularly engaging."

Her eyes lit up, clapping her hands in anticipation. "Excellent. I can hardly wait to cast a spell on him."

Jax giggled, already feeling sorry for the young man. He had no idea what was coming for him.

"Your Grace?" A steward entered the room, bowing as he interrupted the group. "It appears Lord Pettraud's guests have arrived at the gates. Shall I send for escorts?"

Jax leaped from her seat. "I believe these gentlemen deserve a royal welcome, don't you, Carriena? Giovanna?" She could tell from their expressions that the young women were intrigued by these potential suitors.

Beckoning everyone to follow her, Jax took Perry by the arm and trailed after the steward. "I am so excited to meet your friends. It will give me a glimpse of the life you led before coming here."

"It was a bleak life, at that." Perry kissed her temple as she chuckled.

Jax decided she needed some fresh air after being cooped up in the palace all day, breezing past the entrance hall and out onto the veranda. The afternoon sun caressed her cheeks, stretching its rays out across the majestic courtyard. From atop the marble stairs, she could see an ornate carriage unloading at the gates of the palace. While not as opulent as her own, she was nonetheless impressed with the regal splendor of the coach. If she hadn't known who her guests were, she might have assumed it carried a ducal ruler.

A beat after their arrival, one of the carriage doors swung open and raucous laughter burst across the garden. It was followed by the appearance of four figures emerging from within.

"Perry, you old cad, is that you?"

Jax's eyebrows nearly touched her hairline at the words. Considering the rank of these young men, she had expected them to follow proper decorum.

Tensing at her side, she could almost feel the embarrassment radiating off of her fiancé. "Excuse me just a moment, my love." Clearing his throat, Perry took the stairs two at a time, racing toward his Pettraudian companions.

"Perry!" His arrival was greeted with a chorus of hoots and shouts, along with considerable roughhousing. Watching the reunion from afar, Jax would have loved to have overheard what words Perry shared with his friends after being separated from them for so long, but as he had respected her private reunion with her friends, she would do the same.

The clamoring died down as the five young lords strode up the immaculately groomed pathway leading to the palace steps. Jax and her friends took this time to properly appraise the new arrivals.

It was hard to determine which one Perry thought Carriena would take to, as all four men were equally handsome in their own right. Even from a distance, their bright amber eyes glinted with mischief, denoting their noble rank.

"May I present to you the Illustrious Duchess Jacqueline Arienta Xavier," Perry said with a sweeping gesture, signaling for his companions to bow in the presence of the realm's most revered leader. "She is joined by Lady Carriena, Crown Princess of Isla DeLacqua, Sir Charles of the DeLacqua Court, and Lady Giovanna of Hestes."

Bowing in greeting, the four men each stepped forward to kiss the Duchess's hand before introducing themselves.

The tallest of the group, with black hair and a speckling of freckles, cleared his throat. "Greetings, Your Grace. It is an honor that we celebrate your betrothal to our dear friend. I am Baron Skander Eveluce."

Jax dipped her chin with a smile. "I am thrilled to welcome you to Saphire, Baron."

He gave her a playful look. "I hope the rumors that you've adopted our moniker for young Pettraud here are true and that you will come to call me Skander."

"Ah, I might have guessed Perry's friends were the source. His father doesn't seem the type to hand out nicknames," Jax said with a chuckle, and she was pleased to see Skander beaming with approval at her joke. Her days at court were so often consumed by stuffy old courtiers that she relished the attention of people her own age.

"Come now, Skan, you're drooling."

The deep, silky voice dragged Jax's focus to the figure it belonged to. His dark, ebony skin heightened the intensity of his amber eyes, and his gorgeous face looked like it had been constructed by an artisan. Perry did have very attractive friends, indeed. Sizing up his impressive muscles rippling under the sleeves of his tunic, she guessed his identity before the words left his mouth.

"Viscount Emyr, Your Grace. Perry's words have not done you justice. How a sod like him ended up with a creature like you…"

As Jax laughed, she could hear Carriena's dreamy sigh behind her. "You are too kind, Viscount, for the real beauty here is my dearest friend Lady Carriena. Have you met?" She skillfully directed Emyr's attention to a suddenly coy Carriena.

As Emyr kissed her hand and murmured seductive words, Carriena flashed a grin of thanks Jax's way.

Turning back to the remaining two arrivals, Jax commented dryly, "That's got to be a record in matchmaking."

"I hope your friend is up for the challenge. My brother can be a handful."

"I was just about to say the same thing of Lady Carriena. You must be Bran, then?" While not as smoldering as his brother, Bran cut an attractive figure. His chin was covered with a well-groomed beard and golden spectacles rested on his strong nose, giving him a look of distinction. If she had to guess, Jax would peg Bran as the more intellectually inclined of the two.

"And that leaves Earl Edmund Windale," she said, turning to the last new face. Even though she didn't know their exact ages, Jax would have been shocked if Edmund was not the youngest of the four. His face still contained a youthful roundness, but his warm smile made him angelically handsome. His brown hair was cut close to his scalp, and while he stood shorter than the others, Jax doubted he would have any trouble holding his own, due to his impressive muscles.

"An honor, Your Grace. I have not been to Saphire since I was a small child. It certainly has bloomed under your rule."

"Well, I'm so glad you all were able to join us." Jax beamed, surveying the group. "Poor Perry has been trapped here by himself for far too long. I do hope you'll make your visits a regular occurrence."

Coming to her side, Perry squeezed her around the waist. "I haven't regretted a minute since I got here."

Skander playfully clutched his throat and pretended to retch. "Oh gag, Perry. I definitely won't be coming back if I'm subjected to this mushiness the entire time."

Raucous laughter sent the birds in the nearby trees into a frenzy, their wings carrying them off to more peaceful nests. "That's what happens to women when Ed enters a room," Emyr said with a smirk, sending the group into a fresh onslaught of laughter.

"Well, why don't we let you get back to your friends, Duchess? Perry has boasted about the countryside enough in his letters that I'm dying to go for a ride and see for myself if he's just been blinded by love." Bran looked at his companions, who nodded their agreement to the suggestion.

"Of course, please, enjoy yourselves. You have the run of the stables." Jax summoned one of her stewards forward to escort the young men to the horses.

Carriena's lips pursed with a pout. "I like horseback riding, Jax. Why don't we join them?" she asked as they watched Perry and his friends swagger away.

Jax held up a hand to silence further protests. "Goodness,

woman, slow down. Let them have a little time to reconnect. *Then* you can have your fun."

Crossing her arms, Carriena sighed. "You're much too patient for my liking sometimes, you know that?"

"It comes in handy when running a duchy. You might want to try it sometime," Jax said, knowing her friend would one day inherit her father's nation.

Carriena's eyes darkened in reply. "I doubt it's a skill I'll ever need."

Before Jax could process her cryptic remark, her other guests diverted her attention.

"Duchess, might we take a few moments to settle into our rooms? Then maybe a tour of the castle?" Charles suggested. "I am most eager to see your legendary archives."

A hand flew to Jax's forehead. "How could I have been so rude? Here I am, dragging you around and I haven't even let you rest!" She looked apologetically to Charles and Giovanna. "I suppose I'm just so excited to see old friends, I forgot my duties as a hostess."

"No trouble at all, Duchess. It has been wonderful catching up with you," Giovanna reassured her, "and once I get my second wind after a quick respite, I hope the fun continues." She looked down the path that the Pettraudians had taken. "I wouldn't mind getting more familiar with Earl Windale." She raised an eyebrow suggestively.

Her brother's face sprouted red with embarrassment. Ever his sister's protector, Jax was sure that was the last thing he wanted to hear.

"I will see you to your rooms. Shall we reconvene in a few hours?"

"That seems more than enough time for us to settle in," Charles said.

"Wonderful. When you are ready, summon any of the palace staff to escort you to the archives. I will meet you there," Jax instructed as she led her friends back inside the elegant palace walls. "I have some business to take care of with Jaquobie that I want wrapped up before the festivities really begin." She felt her mood dampen slightly at the prospect of the upcoming argument she and her High Courtier were bound to have over tax trades.

She escorted her small party to the guest wing, showing each their selected apartment for the duration of their stay. Carriena's lady's maid was already busy unpacking the bursting trunks stacked neatly in the young woman's cavernous room.

"Did you bring enough? How long are you planning to be here, exactly?" Jax asked, astonished that her friend's carriage had been able to move with all her luggage.

With a shrug of her shoulders, Carriena stretched out across the massive sofa in the sitting room area. "Who knows? Since I'm on the continent, I might as well drop in on a few of the other duchies. It has been ages since I've been to a Zaltorian bazaar."

Bidding farewell to her lovingly obnoxious friend, Jax showed Giovanna and Charles to their respective apartments. "I will see you in the archives in what, three hours? Feel free to take your time, for the welcome feast will not be until after dark."

With that, Jax gathered her skirts and headed toward her personal wing of the palace. Her study, which had once belonged to her father, overlooked the sprawling gardens, in full bloom this time of year. The huge windows letting in the much-needed sunlight to brighten the space were also a huge distraction for Jax, as the sight outside was often too beautiful for her to concentrate.

Sinking into her plush chair, she reviewed the stack of parchment that never seemed to diminish on top of her grand desk. Flipping through the pile, she decided to start with the reports from the outlying towns.

A little over a month ago, several villages in Saphire had held their first-ever elections, appointing local leaders who would oversee the immediate needs of their people. It was all a part of the new era sparked by Darian's ascension to the Cetachi throne. Jax had taken it upon Saphire to test these methods within the borders of her own duchy, with the hopes that other regions would soon adopt the policies.

To her surprise, the first few weeks had been a pleasant success. Instead of sending her courtiers away from the palace to visit each township to hear petitions and resolve ongoing issues, the village leaders were now positioned to handle these matters themselves on a daily basis. She required them to send a weekly summary to the palace for review, an oversight tool to prevent the premiers from abusing their newfound power and influence. Jax still dispatched her courtiers to ensure that these reports aligned with what was really going on in the region and to observe how Saphirians were coping with this change. She actually found it all quite refreshing. She could now wholly focus on protecting her people and expanding Saphire's holdings within the realm.

Reading about a few land disputes in Roderick, one of the smallest villages in the duchy, Jax was pleased by the eloquent manner in which Premier JonLuque resolved the issue and reported it to the palace. His natural ability to lead and care for his own people was the very heart of this whole experiment.

"Is that the Roderick report? They seem to be doing quite well thus far."

Jax lifted her amethyst eyes from the page and greeted the unannounced intruder with a tight smile. Jaquobie rarely knocked when he entered her study.

His towering, rail-thin frame was hidden beneath embroidered robes that signaled his station as Saphire's supreme High Courtier and Jax's senior political advisor. Even though their personal history was somewhat turbulent, as he had often chastised and berated her as a child, she valued his political knowledge above all others. In recent months, after his engagement and subsequent marriage to Lady Lysette, sister to the Duke of Lysandeir, Jaquobie's uptight and frosty exterior had begun to melt slowly. *Very* slowly.

"I trust you have made sure courtiers have been assigned to our guests?" she asked, not bothering with his question.

He bowed his head, a curtain of midnight hair falling in front of his piercing amber eyes. "Of course, Your Grace. With instructions to report back any and all information gathered throughout the day."

Jax cocked a frown. "I don't think we need to be spying on our guests, Jaquobie. These are my friends we are talking about."

"Forgive me, Your Grace, but seeing as we are unfamiliar with Lord Pettraud's companions, I think it best to keep an eye on things for a while," he replied with the finesse of a true statesman.

Jax couldn't help but wonder if Jaquobie was also concerned with whom *she* had chosen to confide in. It was no secret that she had been betrayed not once, but twice, by a woman who had been like a sister to her in her youth. "If you truly think it's necessary. I expect you to alert me if you notice anything of concern."

Jaquobie took his usual seat in a chair by the magnificent stone fireplace that dominated the room. "Of course. Now, to the taxes on trade."

Jax's nose wrinkled with displeasure. During its first six months of nationhood, Cetachi had not been subjected to taxes on goods while it developed into a full-fledged duchy. However, Jaquobie had received word that the other leaders of the realm deemed this goodwill period to be at an end and were implementing tax measures on the newest nation. With her close ties to Darian and Annette and the expert economic insight she had honed at the Academy, Jax was hesitant to charge the fledging duchy at the same tax rate the other, more established regions paid.

"I know that look," Jaquobie commented with surprising warmth. After the role Jax had played in his engagement to Lysette, his shrewd and seemingly unpleasant attitude toward her had softened. "You don't want to tax them yet, do you?"

Jax steeled herself for his disapproval. "I just think that six months is not enough time for them to develop a secure treasury that can offset taxing costs." She stood up from her seat and walked over to the fireplace mantle. "But I also do not want it to appear that I'm showing favoritism because of my familial ties to Annette."

"I agree that we want to veer away from playing favorites," Jaquobie responded, pressing his tented fingertips together in thought, "but I also think you are right about putting too much pressure on their treasury upfront. It would bankrupt the nation before it even had a chance. What if we institute a lighter, startup tax in which Cetachi won't pay the rate the other nations do for, say, two years?"

Jax was astonished at his generosity. "Married life suits you, sir," she teased. "Do you think we could get the other rulers to fall in line, too? If Saphire is the only one to abstain from the regular tax rate, it won't make much of a difference."

Her High Courtier stroked his long, twisted beard. "Mensina would no doubt agree, considering your grandfather has just as much at stake here as you do," he said, then paused for a moment. "I'm sure Lysette can be leveraged to persuade her brother to join. In fact, the only one I'm worried about is DeLacqua."

Jax's eyes widened. "Really? Why?"

He shrugged. "I've heard rumors that the Duke's treasury is a bit low itself. With all the money he is spending shipping goods from the continent, the isles are bleeding gold. He'll take any opportunity to secure a heftier purse."

"Are you certain? Carriena hasn't mentioned a thing." Feeling a knot of hesitation blossom in her stomach, she met Jaquobie's calculated gaze. Did he really believe Carriena was attending her wedding for more devious reasons?

He waited a moment before answering, as if aware he was heading into sensitive territory. "I would exercise caution around her, Jax," he said in a more familiar manner than usual. "Duke DeLacqua's pains are real, and if he sees an opening to exploit his daughter, he will take it. No matter what."

Jax shivered at the hidden threat now looming in her mind. She couldn't possibly imagine Carriena doing anything to jeopardize their friendship, but then again, she had misjudged loyal faces before. "I appreciate your candidness, Jaquobie, but I really hope you're mistaken. I'll draft a proposal for a startup tax, suggesting we wean Cetachi onto the tariffs to avoid an economic collapse. See that it gets delivered, will you?"

Jaquobie nodded. "In person, while the dukedoms are here for the wedding celebrations?"

"Oh no, send them by messenger." Jax waved a hand with disdain. "I don't want my wedding to turn into a trade summit. I'll give Darian the loan from my own personal reserves if it keeps Cetachi afloat through the event."

Her advisor's eyes narrowed. "Don't let your guests overhear offers like that."

"Considering the influx of security around the palace with all the visiting delegations, I'd have to have words with Captain Solomon if anyone got close enough to my private study to eavesdrop on our conversation," she replied, dismissing his concern.

"Courtiers are employed for their ability to obtain useful

information. I'd be cautious if I were you, Jax. Even in your own chambers, the walls are always listening."

She was surprised by the genuine apprehension lacing his words. "Captain Solomon's main task this week is protecting the royal wing. The Ducal Guard has been ordered that the area is off limits to anyone foreign. Even my grandfather and Annette are prohibited from my wing during their stay."

Jaquobie managed to look mildly impressed. "I doubt the Duke will take that well."

"I'm hoping that our stewards will keep his goblet full of mead to keep him thoroughly distracted." Reaching for a quill, she found herself staring at a blank scroll of parchment. "Now, if there's nothing else at the moment, I'll get to work drafting the tariff agreement. We'll reconvene our sessions after the wedding."

Jaquobie's eyebrows rose. "You and Lord Pettraud don't intend to seek seclusion somewhere after the celebrations? Enjoy marital bliss for a week or so?"

Jax laughed. "I know you and Lysette had a lovely trip to the Savant coast, dear sir, but unfortunately, I do not have the luxury of shying away from court. Especially with this Cetachi ordeal."

"The realm would survive you taking a few days of rest, Jax."

If someone had told her a year ago that Jaquobie would encourage her to take a romantic getaway, she would have thought them insane. "It might. But a lot can happen in a few days, and with my attention focused on the wedding, I'm already loosening the reins on the realm enough."

Jaquobie's slender shoulders hunched in a sigh. "Very well. I'll tell Lysette I did my best to persuade you, then."

Ah, the source of all this concern, Jax thought with a smile. She had to admit, she'd grown fond of Jaquobie's new bride. "I'll have the tariff proposal delivered to your rooms shortly," she said in dismissal.

With a bow, the High Courtier left her to her work. As tiresome and particular the drafting of such an agreement was, it felt good to put her mind to work, forcing her burgeoning anxiety to the back of her mind. She supposed that all brides felt a modicum of worry as their wedding day approached, but there seemed to be so much riding on this event.

It would be Darian Fangard's first royal reception since his ascension to the Cetachi throne and all eyes would be on him, scrutinizing every political and social maneuver. There was also the matter of Perry's father attending the festivities. His relationship with his youngest son was still in a fragile state, causing Jax to worry that the exposure Perry would be subjected to this week might actually damage the little progress he'd made when he'd last seen his father.

She also had to admit to herself that she was worried about Uma. Considering this was her first true test as a lady-in-waiting, the Duchess prayed the pressure wouldn't break her dear friend. She believed Uma to be entirely capable of handling the details of the event. What worried Jax was whether her friend would be able to turn a deaf ear to the multitude of gossip that would no doubt follow her around. Witnessing firsthand Lady Carriena's rigidity on the subject, Jax could imagine what the other foreign dignitaries might be saying about Uma's appointment to the esteemed position.

Rubbing her temples, Jax felt the pressure build as her negative thoughts multiplied. Perhaps hosting a lavish wedding in the wake of all the recent changes in the realm had been a foolish notion.

"No, Perry and I deserve this," she said to the empty room.

Chapter Three

A light tap at the door pulled Jax's attention from the pile of papers, a smile slipping across her face as Perry walked in.

"Hello, lovely," he said, cupping her face in his palms.

"How goes it with the boys? Causing chaos already?" she responded with a mischievous grin.

Perry perched on her desk, careful not to muss with her papers. "They seem much more tame than I remember. They all begged off to rest in their rooms before dinner." He looked around the study, rolling his eyes. "Perhaps old age is setting in."

A shadow of worry flitted across her face.

"Don't worry, Jax. I left them in the care of their handlers. I doubt they are up to anything devious at the moment." He placed a reassuring kiss on her forehead.

Blushing at her transparency, Jax stood up and shuffled around the desk to stand directly in front of him. "You know it's nothing personal, Perry. Jaquobie insisted everyone be put on watch. Even Carriena has a courtier reporting her every move."

He took her hand and squeezed it gently. "I know. You don't have to defend your actions to me. You must do whatever is necessary to keep our duchy safe."

She warmed at his words. "'Our duchy'. I like the sound of that."

Perry chuckled. "Well, I guess it's really *your* duchy. I'm just here to look pretty by your side." He gathered her up in his strong arms. "But I do hope you know I consider this home, my love. For the first time in my life, I feel like I've finally found where I belong."

"I've already agreed to marry you, Perry. You don't have to keep buttering me up," she replied with humor but her heart glowed from his admission.

He grinned, knowing his words had been well-received. "We are getting married, aren't we?"

"Yes, you buffoon. And unless you want the pews to be empty, I suggest we go attend to our guests so they know how important they are to us," Jax said, taking his hand and leading him out the door of her study and into the hallway. "I said I would meet Charles and Giovanna at the archives to give them a tour."

They strolled hand-in-hand through the halls, basking in the quiet, knowing it would not remain that way for long.

"Will Lady Giovanna be performing at tonight's feast?" Perry asked as they neared the grand doors of the Saphirian archives.

Jax paused. "I hadn't thought to ask her, with her being a guest and all. But wouldn't that be a treat?" She stroked her chin, a mischievous grin spreading across her face. "Perhaps her voice would cast a spell over Earl Windale."

Perry looked pleasantly surprised. "She's interested in Edmund, you say?"

"She's intrigued by him, to say the least."

"Well, he did mention her beauty more than once during our ride." Perry wiggled his eyebrows suggestively.

"I can only hope for Carriena's sake that Emyr did the same?" Jax asked, her eyes radiating with hope.

Perry answered with a snort. "He's composed their wedding announcement already."

Her giggles echoed down the hallway.

‡

Charles and Giovanna arrived at the archives with their appointed courtiers, their amber eyes bright and alert.

"I hope you've had enough to time rest, because we have quite the exploration planned out for you," Jax said, rubbing her hands together in anticipation. It had been so long since she'd had the time to show off her regal, renowned home to friends.

Giovanna nodded. "I usually don't sleep well when I'm away from my own bed, but I must say, my suite is quite stunning. I would have slept the whole afternoon away if Charles hadn't come to fetch me." She looked at her brother for his response, but his attention had already been captured by the expansive library stretching out before them.

"There is no question in my mind why you are considered the envy of the realm, Duchess," he said with utter fascination, his eyes rapidly scanning the rows and rows of scrolls and manuscripts that reached nearly to the vast ceiling.

The warmth in her chest reflected the pride in the Duchess's face. "Our scholars have been curating this library since the time of the Rebirth," Jax explained. She managed to mask the slight disappointment she felt from the archives not containing more knowledge about the time before the Realm of Virtues was founded.

"Am I correct in remembering that your court physician is a former priest of the Ancient Faith?" Charles asked, his eyes lit with intense interest.

Her bristling reaction was immediate and involuntary, and she regretted it at once. "Yes, Master Vyanti is a member of the Ancient Faith," she responded, hoping her tone sounded neutral. Considering how she had chided Carriena for her prejudices toward Uma and Darian, she felt hypocritical about the negative thoughts clouding her judgment when it came to the Ancient Faith. She had been brought up to be a Child of the Virtues, trusting in the principles of kindness, humility, bravery, and intelligence. The Ancient Faith was an archaic religion, believing that gods and demons ruled over natural life, a faith that was eventually subdued when the people overthrew their oppressors, founding the Realm of Virtues.

Master Vyanti had once been a priest of the Ancient Faith, and he'd long lectured Jax and her family that the religion had been reformed since the days of the Rebirth. Trusting the old man, Jax's father had promoted tolerance of the faith throughout the realm, as some duchies still maintained temples dedicated to the old gods.

Following in his footsteps, she allowed the Ancient Faith to continue its practices within her borders, but she personally didn't have to like it.

Unaware of the storm he'd drudged up inside her mind, Charles innocently continued, "I would love to be able to shadow his practices whilst I am here. Not that I am not learning much from my master in Isla DeLacqua, but Vyanti is a legend amongst the physicians' guild."

"Then Uma must arrange a time for you to speak. I, for one, am hopeful that there won't be any work for you to shadow. I'd hate for anyone to fall ill during the celebrations," Jax commented with wry humor, but the truth of her words rang clear.

As if speaking her name magically summoned her, Uma appeared in the gaping doorway. "Your Grace? Might I remind you that the banquet is set to start in two hours?"

Jax gave her a blank look. "Yes?" A moment passed before Uma's words registered in her brain. "I really need two hours to get ready?"

"It gives you ample time to prepare," Uma said with careful consideration.

As her lips drew into a thin line, Jax turned to her guests, a deep frown set across her face. "Well, that takes the wind out of my sails. It seems I'm being summoned to my chambers to prepare for the evening. Conrad!" She motioned to one of the seasoned palace scholars milling about the room. "See to it that my guests are given a proper tour of the castle, please."

Perry held up a hand. "Jax, why not let me do it? I don't need as much time to get ready for tonight. I'm happy to show Charles and Giovanna our home."

Her stomach flipped at the way his voice caressed the words *our home*. After a quick look at the scholar she had summoned, Jax turned to the siblings. "I hope you don't mind if Perry shows you the lay of the land."

"Of course not, Your Grace," they both said in unison.

"We shall see you at the feast," Giovanna said with a wave as she and Charles moved toward the door to give the couple some privacy.

"I'll try not to give away too many palace secrets." Perry's lavender eyes twinkled with mischief.

Jax responded with an impish smack on his arm.

"I'll come collect you before dinner, so we can peek in on the chapel to make sure the lighting is just right," he said, bestowing a soft kiss to her blushing cheek. He gave her a wink before hurrying away to join his guests.

Jax felt Uma's eyes on her. "I don't think I need to remind you, Your Grace," Uma said, hesitation written all over her face, "but with all the guests we have in the palace…"

"I'm not allowed to have any fun," Jax said, her eyes glowering with annoyance, disappointed she couldn't even show her friends her ancestral home. "I thought I'd be able to sneak in a few hours as a carefree hostess, but between Carriena and the Cetachi delegation already being here, I have to remind myself that being Duchess comes first."

Uma cringed, her small body shrinking beneath Jax's gaze. "I'm sorry."

"I'm not blaming you, dear one." Jax tucked a strand of honeyed hair behind her ear, her fingers brushing the side of her jeweled crown. "I just don't know if I'm ready for all this."

"What do you mean?"

Jax suddenly felt like a boulder had been dropped on her shoulders. "To be the center of everyone's attention. To have all eyes on me. Everything I do will be analyzed and criticized. How is that a good way to begin a marriage?"

Uma's delicate hand rested on her arm. "You've been the center of attention before, Jax. You'll be fine."

"Not really. I mean, my coronation was still laced with the deaths of my parents, so even then I was not the focal point. And since? I have attended many events, yes, but as a guest, an observer. Never as the main attraction."

"When are you ever *not* the main attraction?"

Uma's teasing pulled a slight smile across her face. "You do know what I mean, don't you?"

Brown eyes narrowed in response. "I get it, Jax, I really do. But I also know you are capable of handling this, which is why I think it's pointless to spend time worrying about it. Everything will be fine. I mean, the worst that could go wrong is that your dress falls apart in front of everyone."

Jax's mouth dropped at the horror of that thought.

"And even then, all people will probably talk about is what a lovely figure you have," Uma said, poking at her trim waist.

Throwing her head back, laughter consumed the Duchess. "I hope you realize you've made life extremely difficult for Monsieur Duval. I'll have him reviewing the seams up until the moment I walk down the aisle."

"I'm fairly certain your tailor has the dress under royal guard." Uma chortled.

Jax rolled her eyes. "I'll bet George loves signing off on those orders," she said, picturing the stoic Captain assigning his men to protect a dress.

"Speaking of George and walking down the aisle..." Uma's voice trailed off as she led the way out of the library toward Jax's bedroom. "Have you asked him yet?"

Jax's face paled. "No. And before you give me another lecture, I just haven't found the right moment. I know I said I was going to when we arrived back home from the Lysandeir summit, but things just got away from me." Since her beloved father was not here to walk her down the aisle at her wedding, Jax had decided to ask George Solomon if he would accompany her.

Having enlisted in the Ducal Guard at age sixteen, George had known Jax since she was nine years old. At first, his entry-level rank meant he did not interact with the ducal family on a regular basis, but he proved his loyalty and courage the day he thwarted the kidnapping of a young Jacqueline. A rogue nobleman named Gabriel Reinbeck had planned to hold the princess hostage, demanding the throne of Saphire in exchange for her life. George had protected the young Jax with a fierceness Duke Saphire greatly admired, and he promoted the boy to his inner circle. George continued to prove his unwavering loyalty over the years, which eventually earned him the title of Captain of the Ducal Guard, the most senior military officer in all Saphire. On top of it all, he was her oldest friend and the closest thing she had to family in Saphire with her parents gone.

"You'd better ask him soon, or he won't have time to find something presentable to wear," Uma said with feigned admonishment, holding open the door to Jax's lavish and grand apartment.

"All right, all right." Jax held her hands up in defeat. "You may send for him once we're finished."

"Of course. Do you need anything further?" Uma asked, clasping her hands before her.

Jax couldn't resist a reflective sigh. "I miss the days when this was you and me."

Uma's features softened, her cheeks growing pink. "As do I, Your Grace. But Vita takes good care of you, no?"

Before Jax could answer, a figure darted into the room. "Duquessa! I was beginning to worry we wouldn't have adequate time," the young woman said, her lilting Savantian accent a mere purr.

Vita Bellarose had recently been selected to fill Uma's old position of lady's maid. Hailing from a small earldom in southern Savant, Vita was the daughter of a noble house that was struggling to keep their vineyard afloat. In exchange for their daughter's services, Jax had provided Sir Bellarose a loan to save his family's business. A loan Duke Savant had refused to give, citing that if his nobles could not manage their money effectively, he did not want them associated with his duchy. However, through Jaquobie's spies, Jax had learned that Duke Savant's own treasuries were floundering, as wine production had decreased in recent years due to dry weather. Since wine was the main export of the small nation, it had been a major blow. As the proclaimed protector of the realm, Jax knew she had to intervene, or risk Savant falling apart. She had bailed out several vineyards nearing bankruptcy in exchange for various favors and agreements. Whether fortunate or unfortunate, the Bellarose vineyard produced a wine too bitter for her tastes, and therefore, Vita's services as her lady's maid had been the outcome.

Tucking her long, dark hair behind an ear, Vita's brow furrowed as she studied Jax. "I still cannot decide whether to put you in purple or green tonight."

Even though their relationship was still developing, Jax was pleased so far by Vita's attention to detail and devotion to her role. She had been hesitant as to whether the daughter of a noble house would find this work to be beneath her station, but Vita genuinely seemed to enjoy her new position. More than once, she had thanked Jax for saving her family's reputation and mentioned how proud she was to play a role in their salvation.

Tapping a long finger on her chin, Vita's amber eyes suddenly brightened. "Oh, I know just the piece!" Dashing out of sight for a moment, she returned holding a voluptuous ball gown.

Examining her lady's maid's choice, Jax smiled. "It will be perfect. I'd nearly forgotten about this one."

"So had I," Vita said, laying out the lavender gown, its hem lined with intricate stitching. Spindle-like vines of emerald ivy wrapped around the bottom of the dress, blending both Saphirian purple and Pettraudian green together. "But with the number of gifts you received when your engagement was formally announced, I suppose something was bound to fall through the cracks."

Jax's fingertips stroked the silky skirt, falling in love all over again with the gown designed by the royal tailor of Pettraud. She had received it as a gift from Perry's youngest aunt, welcoming her to the family. Duke Pettraud was the oldest of five siblings, and with his seven sons, his line was one of the largest in the realm. Where Jax had been an only child, nearly unheard of in a ducal line, she was curious to know what it felt like to be a part of such an expansive family tree.

"Shall I prepare a bath?" Vita's question broke through her thoughts.

"Yes, that would be lovely," Jax answered, sinking down into a plush armchair.

‡

Vita had just finished tucking a gold and amethyst crown into Jax's caramel curls when a knock sounded at the door. She rushed over to open it, almost tripping on an ottoman in her path.

Jax concealed a snort behind her raised hand, finding Vita's lack of grace at times to be quite endearing.

"Captain Solomon! Yes, we've just finished," Vita exclaimed

from the apartment door, beckoning Jax to leave her bedroom vanity and greet her friend.

George Solomon stood tall with his hands behind his back, giving Vita a curt bow of thanks as he walked into the room. Spotting Jax, he grinned, his handsome face lighting up. "You look breathtaking."

With a subtle nod to Vita to give them some privacy, Jax floated over to his side. "Thank you, George. Why don't you take a seat?"

"Oh, dear. Am I in some type of trouble?" he joked, but she could tell she'd just put him on alert.

"What's this I hear about you wasting resources by guarding my wedding dress?" she asked, striving to keep her face blank and unreadable.

George shifted in his seat. "Well, Monsieur Duval requested protection, and even though his claims about sabotage seem farfetched, I'd rather be safe than sorry."

Her stony façade crumbled, and she burst into giggles. "Sabotage? He really thinks someone is going to attack my dress?" She quickly gained control of her laughter, worried that tears might spring from her eyes and ruin her carefully applied rouge.

The tension in George's shoulders seemed to deflate as he sank back into his chair. "One can never be too careful when it comes to high fashion, Duchess," he said with a smirk.

"I guess so," she mumbled. "But in all seriousness, do you have any concerns about our guests?"

George's dark eyebrows lifted in question. "Do *you* have any concerns? From what you've told me, the ones I'm worried about won't be arriving until tomorrow."

Jax knew who he referred to. With Dukes Crepsta, Pettraud, and Mensina all set to arrive within a day's time, George was no doubt preparing his men for some of the realm's most formidable leaders. While relations with Mensina and Pettraud were strong, Crepsta's alliance had weakened ever since the Duke's nephew had conspired to commit treason and overthrow Saphire in his name. While Jax and her advisors wanted to believe in Crepsta's resolute support, the whole incident had cast a shadow over the smallest of Saphire's neighboring duchies.

Then there was the small matter that the rest of the realm's leaders would be arriving the day of the rehearsal reception. Jax had extended the invitation to the rehearsal dinner to all the visiting dignitaries, meaning George and his guardsmen would be responsible for securing the safety of the entire realm. A daunting task, indeed.

Feeling his eyes scanning her face for any indication, Jax shook her head. "It's foolish, really. Muddied thoughts put into my mind by Jaquobie. He doesn't necessarily trust Carriena's motivations for being here. Apparently, Isla DeLacqua is having treasury issues."

"That seems to be a growing trend in the realm," George mused, clearly referring to Savant's money troubles.

"It makes me wonder how secure our way of life is."

He looked surprised. "You think the people will exploit this and use it to overthrow the ducal families?"

"It's been on my mind since the peace summit. While I agree we did what was best for Cetachi, I wonder if Darian's ascension to the throne has planted the seed of rebellion in some of the weaker domains. I mean, if a man can't keep his own reserves full, does he really have what it takes to rule a dukedom?"

"Those are dangerous words, Jax," George said, his tone reprimanding. "Ones that I suggest you keep to yourself whilst you have guests within your walls."

"I haven't even shared my concerns with Perry," Jax admitted, wanting to assure George that she knew better than to speak so flippantly about rebellion. "But I wanted you to be on alert about the changing landscape."

"What will you do if Savant or Isla DeLacqua is thrown into civil war?"

Jax shuddered at the notion. "There's a difference in what I want to do versus what I can actually do."

George gave her an assessing gaze. "What do you want?"

She folded her hands in her lap. "What I want is to unite the realm under one banner, led by a sovereign who won't bankrupt her own people."

His words came out as a whisper, his breath stunned from him. "You want to rule the Realm of Virtues yourself?"

"Before you think me a power-hungry fool, hear me out. I admire Darian's way of running a duchy. I've found the elected premiers to be entirely capable of the day-to-day issues facing their people. In my perfect world, those elected officials would report to the overseeing governor of the region, who would then report to me. As Queen."

Chapter Four

George's whistle bounced off her sitting room walls.

"The realm would be funded from one treasury. All taxes would go to the security of the realm, ensuring no nation goes without. The more I think about it, with the way things are being run by my peers, our people would be safer this way," Jax stated. "Of course, this is all entirely theoretical. I could never act upon it."

"But if you had Pettraud, Mensina, and Cetachi backing your claim, who knows what you could accomplish?" George looked at her, the suggestion in his eyes.

Jax flicked a hand. "Again, these are just musings of a woman whose head is getting too big for her own good."

"Your concerns about the health of Savant and Isla DeLacqua are valid, Jax. If there is to be prosperity across the realm, we can't have duchies defaulting."

"A discussion for another day, George. I've gotten us way off topic." She took his hands in hers, meeting his gaze. "The real reason I asked Uma to send you up here is that I have an important favor to ask you."

"A favor?" George's forehead furrowed.

"You see…" Jax trailed off, trying to find the right words to convey her request. "I have always valued my father's incredible instincts, mainly because he saw your potential when you were just a boy. Not a day goes by when you don't devote your entire life to the service of my family. I know you would do anything for this duchy, as I was there the day you put your life on the line to rescue nine-year-old me from Gabriel Reinbeck's assault without a second's hesitation. That was the day you became a member of my father's inner circle, and more importantly, an honorary member of the Xavier family." Jax's throat caught, her eyes tearing up. "You have been by my side for many years as a protector and friend. With my father absent, I would be honored if you would walk me down the aisle on my wedding day."

George's brown eyes pooled with emotion. "Jax, it is I who would be honored," he managed to say, his voice raw.

Beaming, she threw her arms around him. "Thank you. You have no idea how much this means to me."

Clearing his throat, George gave her a tight squeeze before pulling away and regaining his normally stoic composure. "Nice of you to give me enough time to find a suit," he said dryly.

"Oh hush," Jax said with playful snark. "A Duchess runs on her own time and no one else's. But I'm sure Uma has something waiting in the wings for you."

Pushing himself up from the sofa, George paced toward the door, his mood back to business. "I need to get down to the banquet hall before everyone starts trickling in. I want to make sure my men and I have a good vantage point for tonight's festivities."

Jax almost wished she hadn't warned him about Carriena. "Oh, I hoped you would be able to sit back and relax tonight before the real trouble rolls in."

George's chuckling rumbled through the room. "With you, Duchess, there's always trouble."

She knew he meant it as a jest, but she couldn't help but wonder what she might be up against.

As George departed her chambers, Perry's figure replaced his in the doorway. "Doling out last minute orders?" he said with a smirk as he waltzed into the room.

She stood, letting her dress swirl to the ground in all its glory. "You know me too well."

As he took in the sight of her, she could see a faint glimmer of lust bubbling in his eyes. "You look divine," he whispered, his raspy voice heavy with desire.

His dark curls had been tamed, and his emerald and bronze suit hugged his toned figure in all the right ways. Smiling, Jax reached his side and took his arm. "I am so proud to call you mine, Perry."

He kissed her on the forehead. "Shall we go take a look at the chapel?"

†

Her eyes shimmered with happiness as she gazed around the vast hall, the dying sunlight creating the ethereal shadows she'd pictured in her mind all along. "It's perfect."

Perry pulled her close. "I would get married in a mud puddle if it meant spending my life with you, but I'm glad this suits you."

Wrapped in each other's arms for a blissful moment, Jax was the first to pull away. "I imagine our guests are waiting for us."

"It would be rude to deny them their meal any longer," Perry said with a chuckle.

Jax placed a hand on her stomach, feeling it rumble underneath her corset. "I think I'll ask Uma to send out the appetizer before I make my welcome address. I don't think I can ignore my hunger pangs any longer."

"Well, then, by all means, we must go before you faint from starvation."

They arrived hand-in-hand at the entrance to the banquet hall, greeted with bows from the stewards who manned the doorway.

"Your Grace, all your guests are accounted for. Shall I announce you?" a steward called Gregor asked.

"Announce us both, if you will. Consider it practice for future occasions." Jax squeezed Perry's arm, feeling giddy. Protocol had always required them to enter separately, Perry first, followed by Jax, but with their marriage, he would inherit the title of Prince Consort, allowing him to enter by her side.

Gregor disappeared through a side chamber that led up to the steward's balcony. From the other side of the sweepingly grand door, she heard him clear his throat, bringing a halt to the chatter in the room.

"Announcing his future Highness, Lord Pettraud, and her Illustrious Highness Jacqueline Arienta Xavier, Duchess of Saphire!"

The massive door parted, candlelight from the regal chandelier flooding their path. Sharing a tender glance, Jax and Perry walked into the hall, their friends swarming to meet them.

"Oh my, I didn't expect to see you until tomorrow!" Jax feigned as much surprise as she could muster as her aunt Annette appeared before her, arms outstretched.

"Oh, don't even bother. Darian can't keep a secret from me to save his life," Annette said with a laugh, wrapping her arms around her niece.

It always startled Jax how much Annette looked like her sister, Jax's beloved mother, Duchess Amaryllis. They shared the same delicate nose, sculpted cheekbones, and beautiful honey-colored hair. Standing before her now, Annette had a youthful glow about her that Jax hadn't seen in many, many years.

The source of her happiness appeared at her side, his expression sheepish. "She has a special way of weeding things out of me," Darian said with a grin.

Jax laughed. "I really don't need to hear the details." Seeing them both blush at her joke, she gave their arms a squeeze. "It makes me so happy to see you like this," she said to Annette, planting a kiss on her aunt's cheek. "I look forward to catching up over dinner."

Turning to her other guests, Jax greeted them all warmly. She felt particular satisfaction at how close Emyr stood to Carriena and how Edmund's eyes never left Giovanna's stunning face.

Uma appeared at her side, leading the group toward the glistening mahogany table, lined with the most well-crafted dining chairs gold could buy.

"Uma, dear, could you please send the appetizers out before the toast? I'm in need of some refreshment before I have to stand up in front of everyone." Jax spoke in a murmur only her lady-in-waiting could hear.

"Of course," Uma replied with a bow, hustling with grace toward the pantry doors.

"Everything all right?"

Hendrie, Perry's loyal friend and valet, appeared out of thin air next to Jax, his gaze trailing anxiously after Uma.

Knowing how much Perry valued Hendrie, Jax had tried to befriend the young man, but always seemed to fall short in her attempts. With his being outspoken and oftentimes rebellious toward her politics, she felt an ever-shifting chasm existed between them. Jax thought Uma's promotion to lady-in-waiting might convince him of her sincerity in trying to change the stark divisions between common-born and nobility in the realm, but Hendrie retained his usual cool demeanor.

"She's just going to fetch the stewards to bring out the first course," Jax replied, unsure why she felt so defensive.

Hendrie's chocolatey eyes narrowed for a moment before he released a slow exhale.

"Is everything all right with *you*?" Jax asked.

In a rare show of comradery, Hendrie blushed as he scratched his straw-colored hair. "I'm actually not sure, Duchess. Uma's been avoiding me lately," he admitted.

Jax's eyebrows shot up. It was no secret that Hendrie and Uma cared for one another, so this news surprised her. "Not to pry, but have you done anything that might have upset her?" she asked, concerned more for Uma than for the young man before her.

Hendrie looked genuinely perplexed. "I've wracked my brain and can't think of anything I've done."

Jax gave him a sage smile. "When it comes to wooing a lady, you're held accountable for the things you *haven't* done as well."

"Well, goodness, how does one ever know how to please a woman?" Hendrie asked with a resigned helplessness.

"You don't." Jax chuckled. "And it keeps us greatly entertained."

Hendrie finally caught on that he was being teased, and his ears reddened. "If it's not too much to ask, Duchess, could you perhaps make sure she's not angry at me?"

Even with all she had on her plate, Jax didn't hesitate. "I'll see what I can wheedle out of her, but you know how private she is."

"Boy, do I ever," Hendrie mumbled just before he melted into the surrounding crowd.

From the head of the table, Jax motioned for her guests to take their seats. Perry took his usual spot on her left, with Darian and Annette on her right. Carriena secured the seat next to Perry, bumping Emyr down a chair.

Jax saw mild displeasure blossom across Charles's face as he watched Giovanna seat herself between Edmund and Bran. She hoped the young man would find time to enjoy himself, rather than minding his sister.

Uma emerged from the pantry, taking the empty chair between Annette and Jaquobie's young wife, Lysette. Lysette had flourished being away from the snowy fortress that had been her home in Lysandeir. Where once she'd been socially awkward and abrasive, she now displayed a relaxed and elegant manner, allowing Jax to understand why Jaquobie had fallen for the crimson-haired beauty.

Once Uma had taken her seat, an army of stewards appeared from the shadows carrying silver and gold trays laden with delicious breads and fruits. Carts followed, bearing plates of mixed greens, grapes, and sliced pears, a traditional salad in Saphire.

Her food had barely settled in front of her before Jax seized a fork and began to eat, signaling the others to do the same. The Pettraudian visitors cast confused glances at each other, clearly expecting a speech as a prelude to the meal. However, those closest to Jax knew that food often took precedence.

Once the growling in her stomach had subsided, Jax dabbed her lips before standing. A hush immediately descended on the crowd, forks and knives laid to rest for the moment.

"Lord Pettraud and I are delighted to welcome you to the first of many joyful evenings in celebration of our wedding," Jax began. "It warms my heart that you all were willing to travel across the realm to visit us, and I hope you treat Saphire as your home for the next few days." She paused, taking the time to beam at each of her guests. "You are always welcome within these hallowed halls," she decreed, her musical voice floating throughout the cavernous room.

"Virtues praised!" In a resounding chorus, everyone raised their glasses to the health and prosperity of the duchy.

Settling back into her seat, Jax looked to Perry for assessment.

"Short and sweet," he said, and kissed her hand.

Having had plenty of downtime during the afternoon, the dinner table was quite rowdy as boisterous personalities multiplied and the empty bottles of mead stacked up. Jax was sure she spied the court sommelier whisking away the fifteenth bottle, only to bring forth another, filling Skander's glass to the brim before moving on to the next goblet.

"Duchess," Skander said, his words slurring, "Saphire seems to be home to the finest wine cellar I have ever had the pleasure of sampling."

Considering all the Savantian vineyards she was currently financing, Jax would not have expected any less. "I'm delighted you are enjoying our stock. I hope we have enough to keep your glass full for the duration of your stay."

Emyr and Bran snorted in an identical manner. "Is that a challenge, Your Grace?" the elder brother asked.

Jax gave a wicked grin. "I've never met anyone who can come close to drinking Lady Carriena under the table."

To emphasize the point, Carriena finished off her glass and waved it in the air. "I'm just getting started over here."

The heated stares between Emyr and Carriena almost made Jax blush. "Well, why don't we soak up the mead with some braised pheasant." Jax gestured for the dining staff to serve the next course.

As she polished off her cherry cordial chocolate soufflé, Jax was grateful she'd had the sense to stop at two glasses of wine. All around her, her guests were in various states of frivolity, but she knew they'd regret the excessive indulgence in the morning.

"A song! A song!" Carriena called, slapping her fist on the table, urging Giovanna to perform.

Skander and the Viscounts joined in the chant. Jax opened her mouth to shush them, closing it when Lady Giovanna popped up from her chair, her face aglow. Considering how the young woman had protested when she was last called for an impromptu performance, Jax was pleased to see the actress throw inhibition to the wind.

By the end of the heartfelt ballad, Jax felt certain that Edmund had fallen head over heels for the singer. If she wasn't mistaken, even Skander and Bran looked interested, causing poor Charles to sink so low in his chair his head could barely be seen.

Good nights were exchanged all around as the group realized that their drinking was finally getting the better of them. Courtiers appeared from the door, escorting—and in some cases dragging—their charges to their suites for the evening.

Jax had the last laugh as Bran tried kissing one of the gargoyle statues adorning the hallway, mistaking it for a flirtatious maiden. "I would have thought your friends could hold their liquor a little better. Did you see how effortlessly Carriena strode out of here?" she teased Perry as he walked her back to her chambers.

Perry failed to conceal a hiccup. "I said they liked a good mead, not that they were good at handling it."

"Well, I hope they all remember the fun we had tonight. I fear I'll be so busy with the ducal delegations that I won't be able to see them again."

Perry held the door open for his beloved. "No one could ever forget you, Jax." He gave her a kiss, albeit a sloppy one.

"You need a bath," she said, pulling her lips away with a giggle. "See that you get one before everyone thinks I'm marrying a barnyard animal."

Grinning like a madman, Perry faded into the shadows as he headed toward his private apartment. In his place, Uma appeared.

"A successful evening, you think?" she asked, looking hopeful.

Jax nodded, drifting whimsically into her sitting room. "Indeed. A sublime job, Uma," she praised. "I hope your winning streak continues."

Relieved, Uma sank into a chair beside her. "I can only pray that the Virtues keep up their end of the bargain."

They sat in silence for a few minutes, enjoying the warmth radiating from their full stomachs.

"Hendrie was asking about you," Jax ventured.

Even though her eyes were closed, a frown settled over Uma's face. "Oh?"

"He thinks you're avoiding him."

Uma snorted. "Well, I am."

Jax sat up, intrigued by the gossip. "What has the poor sod done?"

Uma shifted in her seat. "Well, it's probably silly…"

"Try me."

Uma opened her eyes and looked to Jax for advice. "He hasn't asked me to be his date at your reception."

Her brow furrowed. "Really?"

"I think he thinks he doesn't have to ask me," Uma admitted. "But he does, right? He can't assume I'd go with him. I mean, I don't know if we're even courting."

Jax sympathized with her friend. It had certainly taken Perry long enough to take a hint. "Why not ask him?"

Uma rolled her eyes. "Oh, what do you know?" she jested. "Your love story reads a bit differently than that of a mere common-born lady."

"Just because my father arranged for Perry and me to wed doesn't mean I don't know a thing or two about courtship," Jax retorted. "If you recall, we fell in love before we made our engagement public."

Uma's grimace told her that she'd made her point. "I'm not the ruler of an entire nation, Jax. I can't just ask a man to be mine exclusively."

"And why the Virtues not?" Jax responded.

Uma's mouth opened but nothing came out. After a moment, she tried again. "Well, I don't know, really. I guess I just want to be asked."

"Ah," Jax said knowingly, "you want to feel desired."

Uma got up and stalked around the room. "Is that so bad?"

"Of course not, dear one. Hendrie's a fool if he doesn't make you feel that way every day. Perhaps I'll pass along some sage advice to Perry that trickles down to him?"

Uma knelt before her. "Oh, Jax, would you? I don't think I have it in me to say it to his face myself."

Jax kissed the top of her friend's head. "I'd be happy to."

Beaming, Uma gathered her skirts and headed for the door, turning around when she reached it. "Thank you so much, Jax. Maybe by the time I get back from the flower shop tomorrow, Hendrie will have some sense knocked into his head."

"The flower shop?"

"Yes, I'm collecting the arrangements for use at the rehearsal dinner ahead of time," Uma explained. "The fireblooms need at least two full days in darkness before they blossom. The florist said if I pick them up tomorrow morning and keep them in the wine cellar, they'll open in time for the rehearsal reception and remain in bloom through the entire event."

"Why not send one of the wedding planners to get them?" Jax did not see the sense in her lady-in-waiting wasting time on such a menial task.

Uma crossed her arms. "I'm willing to trust them with some things, but fireblooms are incredibly rare and require a careful hand. I'd rather see to it myself, given the significance of the flower."

The exotic orange-and-yellow fireblooms had been on display at every ducal wedding since Saphire's founding. Just thinking of her parents surrounded by the same flower during their marriage celebrations made Jax feel as though they were with her in spirit. "I can't wait to see them. Did you know it is a royal decree in Saphire that fireblooms cannot be used for any purpose other than a wedding?"

Uma's lips pursed. "A bit selfish, really."

Jax dismissed the taunt. "I've never seen one myself before. Perhaps you can give me a secret preview when you arrive back home?"

Uma shook her head. "Oh no, they will be kept under lock and key, away from *any* prying eyes until the rehearsal reception," she said pointedly.

"Fine, have it your way then." Jax shooed her away. "Good night, Uma."

"Sleep well, Jax. Only three nights left before you'll move to your new chambers with your husband," Uma trilled, waving goodbye.

Jax shuddered, a sudden unease filling her chest. Uma was right. These rooms would no longer be her home once she and Perry married. Over the past few months, Uma had been overseeing the renovation of Jax's parents' apartment, which would soon belong to her and Perry. Jax had resisted the move for so long, as she felt it disrespectful to disturb the memories tied to the royal chambers, but the newlyweds would need more space than Jax's current suite offered.

Vita emerged from the door connecting her service chambers to that of her charge. "Duquessa, I trust you had a pleasant evening?"

Nodding, Jax remained silent as her lady's maid went to work removing the layers of makeup and brushing the curls from her hair.

Within a half hour, her gown was tucked safely away and Jax lay in her canopy bed, staring out the window. Stars infused the sky, lulling her into a peaceful dream.

Chapter Five

"Stop fidgeting so much, Perry," Jax said as she slapped his hands away from the gold buttons of his uniform. "Everything is going to be fine."

"Is it really, though?" He cursed under his breath, and Jax noticed he had resumed tapping his foot impatiently on the marble floor.

A Pettraudian courtier had arrived at the castle gates a few moments ago, heralding the approaching envoy transporting Duke Pettraud. Considering they had not been expecting the Duke to arrive until well after lunch, Jax and Perry hastily excused themselves from a late breakfast to go greet the party.

"Did Emyr and Bran seem like they were still drunk to you?" Perry asked.

Jax chuckled. "Even if they are, that does not reflect poorly on you. Didn't you say your father arranged for your meeting in the first place?"

Her words did little to soothe him. "He'll find a way to berate me. You'll see."

She patted him gingerly on the arm. "Well, I'll make sure Uma keeps them hidden away as soon as she returns from the Sephretta market." The capital city's greenhouse was the only place in Saphire that cultivated the fireblooms.

Perry tensed beside her as the heavy gates to the courtyard swung open, his father's imposing shadow preceding his towering figure.

The familial resemblance is astounding, Jax thought as Duke Pettraud marched up the lengthy cobblestone path.

Bowing low, the Duke's forest green cloak swirled around his muscular build. "Duchess Jacqueline, my sons and I are pleased to be in your lovely capital. I have forgotten how beautiful Saphire is in the spring."

Jax extended her hand, and the Duke respectfully kissed it. "I am delighted you are here to share in our joy, Duke Pettraud." She turned her focus to the three men standing behind him. "And I welcome my new brothers to our home."

Duke Pettraud waved them forward to be introduced. "My eldest son and heir, Philippe, Your Grace."

Philippe bowed low, his smirk unmistakable. This was clearly a man who relished being his father's favorite. Unlike Perry and the Duke, he had long, wispy blond hair, so light it was almost white. Jax thought his chiseled features and large, wide eyes were reminiscent of Perry's mother.

"This is Elias, my second born," the Duke continued, pointing to the largest of the three. While not exactly overweight, he was bulky and thick. Elias's hair appeared dark, like Perry's, but it was shaved so close to his head that she couldn't be sure.

"And this is Kaul, my second youngest."

Jax put his age at two, maybe three years older than Perry. Out of the three, he resembled Perry the most, yet Kaul possessed a remarkably lanky and underweight build. Jax feared a gust of wind might blow him over.

"Percival, you're looking well," the Duke said, finally acknowledging his son for the first time.

Considering Perry was about to marry the leader of the strongest nation in the realm, Jax would have thought his family would demonstrate more acceptance, perhaps even appear impressed. In moments like these, she wondered why Duke Pettraud had put forth his youngest son as a marriage candidate when the negotiations had gone on with her father if he so obviously preferred his other sons.

"Hello, Father," Perry said with an equal amount of warmth. "Brothers, good to see you all looking well." His eyes held an expression reminiscent of physical pain as he stood before them.

Philippe, who Jax estimated to be Perry's senior by a good fifteen years, nodded. "It has been too long, young Percy."

Perry failed to conceal a cringe at the name and Jax wondered the reason behind it.

Before the situation became any more frosty—Jax felt enough of a chill to ruin her prized gardens—she came to Perry's rescue. "I shall have my stewards escort you all to your private wing. My home is yours whilst you are here."

"I hope you had the sense, Jacqueline, not to stuff me in a tower full of courtiers," the Duke said with a grumble.

It shocked Jax to realize he was teasing her. "I, for one, know that you belong in the premier guest suite, Your Excellency." It seemed Duke Pettraud had yet to forgive a slight committed by his host during the Lysandeir peace summit.

As the stewards assisted the accompanying valets with the bags, Jax searched for a topic to break the tense silence. "How are the rest of your children? It's a shame they couldn't all be here to celebrate," she said to the Duke.

He stroked his chin, his lavender eyes darting to Perry. "They are well, thank you, Duchess."

Well, I guess that is that, Jax mused as her stewards led the way to the guest suites reserved for Pettraud. She watched as the Duke and his sons were swallowed up by the palace, Jaquobie's courtiers trailing them a respectful distance.

Turning to an ashen Perry, she reached for his hand. "What on earth was going on between you all?"

Growling, he stalked away, forcing her to follow him deep into the lush gardens.

"Perry?" she asked once more.

Dropping down onto a bench, his placed his head in his hands. "We shouldn't have invited them, Jax. My father, yes, but my brothers…they don't need to be here."

She sat down beside him, patting a comforting hand on his back. "Darling, what has gotten into you?"

"They'll just try to ruin everything and make it all about them," he complained, his voice muffled by his hands.

She decided to wait for him to share more, and it only took a few minutes of strained silence before he broke.

"I mean, Philippe has already started after it," he said with venom. "He knows, as they all do, that I don't go by Percy anymore."

"Why not?" Jax didn't see anything wrong with the nickname, although he'd never mentioned it to her before now.

"It was my mother's name for me when I was little. She doted on me so much that when she wasn't watching, they would take her handbags and beat me with them, yelling 'Purse-y, Purse-y' over and over again." He shuddered at the memory.

Jax bit her lip. Perhaps being an only child, she didn't truly understand the trauma behind the taunting, for to her it seemed like something Perry could easily look beyond. "Could it be his way of honoring your mother's memory, by using that name now?"

Perry's eyes darkened. "I highly doubt it." He looked at his entwined hands. "After she was buried, I remember him telling me that no one would ever love 'Mother's little Percy' again."

Jax scowled at the remark. "For Virtues' sake, you were both grown men when that happened. Why would you let that bother you?"

Turning his back to her, he stood up with his hands in his pockets. "I know you're trying to help, Jax, but you just wouldn't understand. Both your parents worshiped the ground you walked on. My mother was the only person in my family who made me feel I was loved. When she died, all that was left behind for me was hatred and disappointment."

Jax moved to his side, placing her hand on his shoulder. "I suppose I don't understand, Perry. I don't understand how anyone could not love you."

His eyes found hers, giving her a small smile. "I learned long ago that I don't need their love or approval to be happy. All I need is yours."

She cupped his cheek in her palm. "And you have it." She rested her forehead against his, breathing in the scent of him. "Shall we enjoy the sunshine a bit longer? How about a stroll?"

He laced his arm through hers and whisked her away.

"I hope your apartments are to your satisfaction, Duke Pettraud," Jax said before popping a soupy crouton in her mouth.

His spoon hovered over the venison stew. "Yes, Duchess, our accommodations are quite sufficient."

She smiled, knowing that was as close to a compliment as she was likely going to get from her future father-in-law.

On her left, Perry absentmindedly stirred his lunch, not having said a word since everyone sat down to the outdoor picnic. The dining hall staff had set up a lengthy wooden table outside, along with enough chairs for the assembled guests. Bran, Emyr, and Skander were noticeably absent, as was Carriena. Jax thought she had heard Hendrie mention to Perry that the group had opted to go for a horseback ride and would have a light lunch when they returned.

Poor Edmund was having a tough time handling the Pettraud brothers without his comrades. After two or three failed jokes, he turned his full attention to Giovanna and Charles, who were animatedly discussing their favorite scenes in their father's plays.

It seemed that Perry and his family preferred the silence between them, so Jax concentrated on devouring her meal so she could escape and find Carriena. She wouldn't mind taking her stallion, Mortimer, for a ride to pass the time until the Crepsta and Mensina delegations arrived.

Placing her napkin down once her soup bowl was empty, she excused herself and nearly ran out of the gardens to escape the brewing family drama. Charles and Giovanna gave her sympathetic looks as she departed, but at least they didn't seem to hold her in-laws' frosty manner against her.

She arrived at the stables a few minutes later, tying up her long hair in a messy bun. Vita would no doubt chastise her for creating unnecessary tangles because of it.

"Hendrie? What are you doing here?" She squinted, realizing the valet was pacing at the head of the carriage path near the elaborate barn.

He looked up, startled. "Duchess, I didn't hear you walk up. I'm waiting for Uma to return. I have something to ask her…" he trailed off.

The corners of Jax's mouth turned up. It looked like the talk she had with Perry while they traipsed around the gardens that morning had done its job. "I think she must be in the cellar attending to the fireblooms."

"I just came from there," Hendrie said with a frown.

"Hmm. Perhaps she dropped off the flowers and grabbed lunch in the kitchens?" Jax offered.

"No, Jax, the flowers weren't in the cellar, either." He crossed his arms and looked down the dirt road. "I don't think Uma's returned from Sephretta."

"She left before breakfast. She should be back by now," Jax murmured in thought, unease running through her veins. "Did she go alone?"

"No, she had two of my men with her," came another male voice. Captain Solomon appeared from inside the barndoor, a beautiful bay mare beside him. "I expected them back at least an hour ago."

Jax looked at the horse's saddle. "What are *you* doing?"

"Going to ride down the path and see if their carriage lost a wheel or something," George answered before hoisting himself onto the animal's back.

Jax didn't like his cryptic use of the phrase 'or something'. Gathering her skirts, she hastened toward the stable. "Well, I'm coming with you."

The Captain opened his mouth to protest but she sent him a silencing look. "I have time before my grandfather arrives, and I need to get away from all the angst brewing between the Pettraud clan." She folded her arms. "Besides, the fresh air will do me good, and it will give me the chance to see the fireblooms."

"I'll come, too!" Hendrie chimed in. "If their carriage is broken, you'll need a few extra horses to help everyone get back to the palace."

George did not look pleased by his growing entourage. "Tack up quickly, then."

As Hendrie ran to fetch the horses, Jax couldn't help but be unnerved by George's demeanor. He wasn't acting like a mere carriage wheel had broken. "Is there something I should know about, Captain?" she asked, her tone brimming with authority.

He looked at her for a moment, as if weighing his thoughts. "Stay close to me, Duchess."

A chill ran down her spine at the veiled warning. "George, is there something wrong?"

"I can't be sure. But Uma has been away from the palace for far too long." His eyes trailed down the carriage path. "I have to admit, I'm worried."

The knot in her stomach tightened.

Hendrie returned a few minutes later with Jax's beautiful midnight stallion in tow.

"Hello, Mortimer," she cooed, rubbing the horse's velvet nose. Given to her by Duke Crepsta and his wife for her eighteenth birthday, he was a treasured gift from the days when their duchies were close allies.

Hendrie had selected a chestnut mare for himself. "Lead the way, Captain," he said, as if he were in charge.

Wishing she was wearing a more appropriate riding gown, Jax hauled herself onto the saddle without assistance. While she hadn't ridden in a while, she'd been trained since birth and was a natural.

George waited for her to situate her dress before urging his mount forward. They took off down the carriage path, and it wasn't long before the leafy trees of the forest obscured the palace from view.

Jax normally did not ride along the road and found she wasn't as familiar with her surroundings as she felt she should be. Most of her journeys took place within the confines of a carriage, so it was a pleasant change to view her duchy from out in the open. Different view aside, she had unhappy memories of the last time she'd ridden Mortimer along this road. Shuddering, she pushed the thoughts of her parents' murder out of her mind.

George, too, would no doubt be reminded of that tragedy, but he kept silent watch as they cantered along the dirt and rock.

After thirty minutes or so of riding, Jax guessed they were more than halfway to Sephretta's city square but still hadn't come across Uma or her guards.

"Wait," George commanded, gesturing for her and Hendrie to halt in their tracks. "Duchess, I order you to stay right where you are. Hendrie, do not leave her side."

It was rare that Jax ever did what she was told, but the quiet dread in George's voice made her shake with fear. "What is it, George?"

He met her gaze, his dark eyes burning. "Jax, I need you to *stay put.*"

Nodding in promise, she gulped, exchanging frightened looks with Hendrie.

Drawing his sword, George kicked his mare forward and headed toward a bend in the road.

Narrowing her eyes to focus on the sight up ahead, Jax gasped. "Virtues, no! Is that one of the palace carriages?"

Nearly hidden amongst the dense foliage ornamenting the side of the road, Jax saw the wheels of an overturned coach spinning with sinister malice in the air. The sight brought forth a visceral reaction. Jax managed to slide to the ground from her horse's back before she was sick.

"Duchess?" Hendrie was at her side in an instant, offering a handkerchief so she could wipe her mouth.

"I'm so sorry," she said, tears threatening to break through. "It's just...this scene...it reminds me...my parents—" she broke off, unable to finish. If anything had happened to Uma all because of some stupid flowers...

"Hendrie! Bring the Duchess to me," George ordered.

Jax leaned on Hendrie, still feeling weak. "George, what's going on?" she whimpered, but he kept quiet until she reached his side. "What on earth happened? *Where is Uma?*" Her voice rose several notes with each word. She couldn't comprehend the destruction she saw just yet.

George's penetrating eyes roamed over the debris from the carriage. Its doors had been ripped off and tossed aside, along with several gilded wood planks torn from the sides. Filling from the cushioned seats inside the coach spilled out onto the ground. Bulbs of orange and yellow flowers were strewn everywhere. "She's not here."

Chapter Six

"**W**ell, where is she?" Hendrie asked, clearly unable to process the scene of chaos before them.

Jax's eyes darted around the leafy grove, trying to figure out what could have happened. Had the carriage overturned, leaving Uma and her escorts to walk back to the palace on foot? If so, why hadn't they passed her on the road?

"Virtues, no." George's dismayed voice floated from behind the wrecked coach.

"What is it?" Jax gathered her dress and climbed over a broken axle to get to the other side.

"Jax, stay back!" George shouted, but it was too late.

Her eyes widened as she took in the sight of a Saphirian guard lying on the ground, his purple and gold tunic covered in blood.

"Is he…?" Jax didn't want to fully voice the question.

"Yes, but not due to a carriage accident." With rage boiling off his muscular frame, George bent down and ripped something from the man's side. "He was murdered."

Jax's searching gaze danced across the small dagger, unremarkable in make or model. "Murdered? George, where is Uma?"

"Oh, heavens," came Hendrie's gasp from the front of the caravan.

"What is it?" George bounded over to the ashen-faced valet. He knelt to the ground, more sorrow building in his eyes. "Oh, no. Preston."

Jax joined them, her blood chilled to her bones by the lifeless face of another guardsman, a wooden arrow protruding from his chest. "Who could have done this?" she seethed, her words a mere hiss on the wind.

"Where is Uma?" Hendrie's pleas were more frantic now.

"Wait here by the carriage while I search the area," George commanded, giving Jax and Hendrie stern looks. For extra measure, he grabbed a small knife from his boot and handed it to Hendrie.

The poor man looked absolutely helpless, so Jax seized the blade for herself. "Be careful, George. The attackers could still be in the area."

With a firm, knowing nod, he disappeared into the underbrush.

Despite the rising panic in her stomach, Jax took a deep breath, chastising herself. She needed to keep a cool head for Uma's sake. Her keen eyes scanned the overturned carriage and two dead bodies, looking for any clues as to who could have committed such a violent crime within her borders.

A fluttering noise on the breeze caught her attention, and her eyes zeroed in on a nearby tree. A piece of parchment, no bigger than a page from a book, flapped in ominous announcement. Held in place by a bloody dagger, similar to the one George had pulled from the first dead guard, it beckoned her forward.

Leaving Hendrie's trembling side, she took careful steps over to the tree, as if she was afraid it might suddenly yank up its roots and scatter. "What's this?" she asked, mostly to herself. With trembling fingers, Jax ripped the parchment away from its sharp peg.

Fluid script tattooed the page, the black ink bleeding into the fibers of the note. As she read the warning, a conflicting surge of relief and fear hit her head on. "George!" she called out to the woods, and within seconds, the winded Captain stood beside her.

"What is it?"

"Uma is alive. She isn't here, but she's alive," she stated, her calm voice detached from the horror welling up in her heart. "Whoever did this left a message behind."

George took the parchment from her shaking hands and read it aloud. *"You have something of ours, so we took something of yours. Now, you can wait."* He looked at her, confusion in his eyes. "What on earth is this supposed to mean?"

"Uma's been kidnapped," Jax said, stating the obvious. She took the parchment from him and examined the intricate scrawl. "I just don't know what I have that these thugs would want." Her gaze dropped down to the hand-drawn signet at the bottom of the note. A shiver flowed down her spine as she examined it. Etched within the drawing of an upside-down shield was a gnarled sword with a crude serpent wrapped around the blade. "Have you ever seen a mark like this before?"

George's eyes narrowed as he searched his memories. "Not that I can recall."

"This isn't a crest belonging to any of the noble families within Saphire," she said with certainty, "but that hardly narrows it down." She glanced at the drawing again. Her blood turned to ice at the sight of the sinister image, and she marveled its unsettling effect on her.

"Someone is out to sabotage your wedding," George guessed.

Jax stared at the haunting message once more. "But what do I have that they want?"

"Besides the throne of the most powerful nation in the realm?" he said dryly.

She shot him a condemning look. "This reads more personal than that."

"Duchess! Captain! Over here!" Hendrie's voice called from the wreckage.

Dashing over as quickly as her dress would allow, Jax reached the valet's side just as George asked, "What is it?"

"Look! I think someone is trapped underneath the tail board." Hendrie pointed with alarm at the broken back of the coach.

With speed and strength, George lifted the heavy board off a cluster of brush, revealing the face of a boy, no older than eighteen, buried beneath the rubble.

"Virtues." Jax knelt beside the unconscious young man, her heart racing. His breath was shallow and quick, but he was indeed still alive. "We need to get this poor lad back to the castle at once. He may be able to tell us what happened."

Although George nodded his agreement, Jax could tell he was at war with himself. "George, you take him and ride ahead. Hendrie and I will keep up as best we can, but it is imperative you get him to Master Vyanti at once."

"Jax, I can't leave you unprotected out here," he objected. "You know that."

"I understand, and I won't be defenseless," she replied, pulling the hilt of his longsword from the scabbard attached to his belt. "You were the one to train me with this when I was a young girl. I know how to use it."

Her brazen action failed to convince him. "Jax, after what these people did to Uma—"

"Exactly. They did this to *my* friend, and I will not let anything get in the way of rescuing her. She's in this predicament because of me." Jax paused, feeling her throat catch with emotion. "This boy is the only clue we have to finding her. I need him alive."

"Saphire needs *you* alive, Duchess." George stood firm, in spite of the certain knowledge that he was poking a dangerous beast.

Just as Jax's mouth opened to force him to obey her command, Hendrie interrupted. "I'm lighter, so I will be able to travel faster with another in tow. I can take the boy back to Vyanti. Please. We're running out of time."

Waging their options for only a moment, George conceded and lifted the unconscious boy from the ground, dragging him toward Hendrie's horse, leaving Jax to stew in her anger.

Her two companions quickly secured the young man's limp form atop the horse, and Hendrie galloped away, a pack of phantom wolves biting at his heels.

Alone at last, Jax turned to George and bellowed. "How dare you defy my direct orders like that." Her tone was vicious.

George met her heated gaze head on. "You must be losing your mind if you think I'm going to leave you to fend for yourself after one of your own was just attacked."

"Watch your tongue, Captain. Might I remind you that I am *your Duchess*?" Jax snapped, furious at having her intelligence insulted.

"No, you don't need to remind me, Your Grace, because I am

doing my job to protect you, which means I have to do what's best for you and *you* alone," George thundered, his face red.

His outburst startled her, causing her to take a step back. "What's that supposed to mean?"

George ran a hand over the close-cut hairs on his head. "You are my responsibility, Jax. My top priority. If I must risk the life of someone else just to keep you safe, then I will do it in a heartbeat."

"Even Uma?" Jax whispered, her chest full of dread.

"Even Uma," he responded sadly.

Jax saw his temper deflate before her eyes. The tears she'd been struggling to hold in broke through her emotional dam, cascading down her face. "If any harm comes her way because of me," she began, her words strangled by gut-wrenching sobs.

George gathered her up into his arms, stroking her hair until she controlled her cries.

"We need to follow Hendrie," Jax croaked.

Nodding in agreement, George led the way to their ever-patient horses. "I told him to speak to no one and to go directly to Vyanti. I don't want word of Uma's disappearance spreading around the castle. With all the different delegations visiting, any one of them could be behind this. Its best if we keep it to ourselves, so that no one is put on alert while my men investigate."

Gripping Mortimer's reins, Jax tossed a look over her shoulder. "You're the one who's lost his mind if you think I'm not going to help you get to the bottom of this," she said with a snort, feeling a spark of hope that all was not lost.

George didn't bother concealing his rolling eyes, taking off in a gallop before Jax could respond.

‡

They arrived back at the castle a little while later, severely winded from the arduous horseback ride.

Wincing as she breathed through a pinch in her side, Jax led the way from the stables to Master Vyanti's chambers deep within the belly of the palace. "Send some of your men back to the carriage, George. If we're going to pretend like nothing is amiss, I need the firebloots brought here immediately and placed in the wine cellar. My guests will notice something's off if no blooms are present at the rehearsal dinner in two night's time." As trivial as it sounded to be worrying about flowers right now, Jax knew that their absence would be a dead giveaway that something had gone wrong.

Without hesitation, George summoned the nearest guardsmen he could find and dispatched them to the forest to collect the flowers, as well as the bodies of the two slain soldiers. "Come now, let's go see if Vyanti has made any progress with our witness."

Jax did not need additional prodding. She followed in George's shadow in a sedate stride, careful not to draw attention to themselves by scurrying through the halls. The Virtues must have been looking down on her, for they did not run across any of her guests along the way.

Master Vyanti's chambers were in the lower recesses of the castle, the warm spring air not yet penetrating the cool passageways. She rarely visited this area of her domain. The memory of her last time here, when the court physician had summoned her to investigate the bodies of her parents, still made her tremble.

Murmuring voices up ahead jolted her thoughts to the present. "Master Vyanti? Is that you?" she called down the dimly lit corridor.

The old man's head poked out of a doorway, his wrinkled face looking shocked. "Duchess? What on earth are you doing down here? What is all this secrecy Hendrie is insisting upon?"

Hurrying the remaining steps, Jax and Captain Solomon strode into the room with purpose. "Close the door, Vyanti," she said as she walked over to the examination table. The injured boy lay upon it, still unconscious, but it appeared that color was returning to his cheeks. "Has he woken up at all?" she asked, looking at Hendrie.

Wiping sweat from his brow, he shook his head. "No, he's been out the entire time."

Vyanti went back to work, his robes sweeping across the floor as he retreated into his medicine cabinet. "Is anyone going to tell me what's going on? Young Hendrie burst in here with this poor boy, but demanded my silence."

Jax shot an approving look at the valet before clearing her throat. "I'm sorry, old friend, for the shroud of secrecy. We're dealing with a bit of an incident I'm afraid." She glanced at George, who gave her an encouraging look to continue. "This young man was found at the scene of a crime. Lady Uma has been kidnapped, and he was the only one we found alive."

"Good spirits! Kidnapped?" Vyanti took a stumbling step backward, clearly stunned by the announcement.

"Yes, and the culprits left very little to go on. I'm hoping our friend here can tell us what happened." Jax motioned to the physician's newest patient.

The elderly man frowned. "Well, Duchess, I hope I can bring him back from the abyss. Whoever attacked him tried to kill him. If the blow to his head had been but an inch lower…" his frail voice trailed off, leaving Jax and her friends to figure out the implications.

She paced nervously around the room, not wanting to interfere with the physician's work but eager to know more about the lad. "Will you be able to help him?"

Vyanti's cloudy eyes examined his charge. "I believe so, but he needs rest. I'll come get you the moment he wakes up."

"Come find me, instead, Master," George ordered with resolute firmness. "We don't want to draw any unnecessary attention to the Duchess until this matter is resolved."

"Of course." Vyanti bowed his head in acquiescence.

Turning to Jax, George motioned to the door. "Your grandfather will no doubt be arriving soon. We need to get you back upstairs."

Bidding the worried physician goodbye, Jax followed Hendrie and George back out into the hallway. "I can't just stand around and pretend like everything is normal with Uma missing!" she hissed, feeling a swell of panic rush through her veins.

"I'm going to ride back out to the caravan and take another look around to see if we missed anything," George replied. "I know it pains you to do so, Jax, but for Uma's safety, you must remain calm. Use that clever mind of yours and see if you can dig up anything from your guests that might be of use."

"You really think someone in the castle might be behind this?" Jax whispered.

George took a moment before responding. "Whoever attacked her knows just how much Uma means to you. I don't think we should dismiss the possibility that they have eyes and ears inside our walls."

Pulling out the threatening letter, Jax read the chilling words once more. *You have something of ours.* What did she have that someone would go to such drastic measures to get back? Some gold artifact in her royal treasury, perhaps? She couldn't help but think back to Jaquobie's veiled warning concerning Isla DeLacqua's financial straits. Would the Duke stoop so low as to hold her lady-in-waiting hostage in return for funding?

"What are you thinking?" George asked, his eyes never leaving her face.

"My mind is spinning out of control right now," Jax said, dismissing the outrageous accusation as quickly as it appeared. "I'm going to keep this on my person." She sighed as she folded the note. "Until the boy wakes up, it's all we have to go on." She tucked the parchment back into the pocket of her dress.

George turned to Hendrie. "See that the Duchess safely arrives at the throne room. I'm going to stop by the soldiers' quarters and arrange for her security to be doubled before I head out and will have them meet you there." He gave the valet a stern look before taking off down the hallway.

Jax placed a hand on Hendrie's arm, noticing his red-rimmed eyes. "How are you holding up?"

"How could something like this happen to her? Uma wouldn't harm a fly."

Jax took no offense that he hadn't answered her question, understanding his thoughts being with Uma. She kept her face neutral for his sake. "We will find her, Hendrie. Of that, I can assure you."

"But we have so little to go on," he said with a whimper.

"We've solved puzzles with less, remember?" She poked at his shoulder, trying to lighten the mood, for it was the only way she would survive the terror building up inside her.

"How am I supposed to keep this a secret from Perry?" he asked, his voice hoarse.

"I'll tell Perry myself," Jax said quickly. "We don't need to keep my future husband in the dark. But not a word of this to anyone else, understand?"

Wide-eyed, Hendrie nodded before dropping his chin in defeat. "It just seems so hopeless."

"We'll find her," Jax repeated. *We've just got to.*

Chapter Seven

Jax and Hendrie walked to the throne room in silence, where she was greeted by six of the most seasoned members of the Ducal Guard.

"I take it you are my new entourage?" Jax asked with wry humor, and the six nodded in reply.

"What's all this about?" Perry asked as he entered the room, confusion written all over his face. "You disappeared for a while there. My family already scare you off?"

Just seeing him made her smile, but as Hendrie visibly tensed at her side, the contented feeling did not last long. "Oh, Perry. There's been a dreadful development."

Taking him into her confidence, Jax brought him up to speed on all that had happened during their brief time away from the castle. His face grew more and more troubled, a deep-set frown marring his handsome features by the time she concluded her story.

He reviewed the threatening note the kidnappers had left behind. "Any idea when this could have happened? How long has it been since the attack?"

"Uma departed before dawn to ride down to the town square," Hendrie answered.

"If she left that early, she should have been back well before lunch," Jax said. "I can't believe I didn't so much as bat an eye when she didn't show up to receive your father." Racked with guilt, she sought comfort from Perry.

He wrapped an arm around her. "With all you've got on your plate, you can't blame yourself."

"If anyone's to blame, it's me. I thought she was just avoiding me again, which is why I didn't seek her out sooner." Hendrie's glum expression pulled at Jax's heartstrings.

"It's the people who did this to our friend who are at fault," Perry said with a growl, forcing Jax and Hendrie out of their self-deprecating moods. "We can reasonably assume the carriage was attacked sometime in the late morning."

"George's men are retrieving the two slain guards. Once Vyanti performs autopsies on them, we'll know for sure." A burst of rage flooded Jax's veins as it sank in that two of her faithful guardsmen had lost their lives in this deadly plot. She was determined that no more harm would come to her people.

Hendrie looked to Perry. "Do you think your father saw anything out of the ordinary while on the road to the castle?"

He shook his head. "No, he and my brothers would have arrived from the western road. That's the most direct route from Pettraud. They wouldn't have gone near Sephretta's city limits."

Pointing down to the bottom of the parchment still in Perry's hand, Jax asked, "Does this crest look familiar to you at all?"

"I've never seen anything so sinister before," he answered.

She wished she could say the same. This wasn't the first menacing threat she'd ever received. "Let's hope George returns with something we missed at the scene or that Vyanti's patient wakes up sooner rather than later." She took the note from Perry and tucked it away once more. "For now, I've got to figure out a way to make it seem like my lady-in-waiting isn't missing." She brushed a speck of dirt from her gown. "I should go freshen up before my grandfather arrives. Come find me at once if you think of something, but for Virtues' sake, be discreet about it."

Perry frowned. "Do you really think it's wise to not alert our guests as to what's happened?"

"If there's someone inside the castle plotting against Saphire, I'd rather have them think they have the upper hand by appearing to be oblivious. It might cause them to slip up and make a mistake," she explained with grim diplomacy before bidding the two farewell.

Jax wished that she didn't have six guards following her as she hastened back to her chambers. She desperately wanted to hide in an alcove and release the burgeoning tears welling behind her eyes. But for her duchy, she had to remain strong. Sovereigns of nations didn't weep in public over a missing member of their court. As much terror as she felt for Uma and what she might be experiencing at the hands of her kidnappers, she knew she had to remain levelheaded if she wanted to get to the bottom of this. With the piece of paper in her dress pocket the only clue, she had so little to go on, it would be a struggle not to feel hopelessness clawing at her heart.

"Duquessa! I wasn't expecting you back until later this evening to prepare for dinner," Vita said in surprise as Jax rushed into her chambers. "Is everything all right?"

Taking a few deep breaths to calm herself, Jax forced a smile. "Just wedding nerves sneaking up on me. I'd like to change before my grandfather arrives, please," she said, quickly switching the subject before Vita could pry more.

Fifteen minutes later, Jax wore a fresh yellow gown with her hair pulled back in a low bun. Vita was wise enough not to ask any questions, despite finding several twigs in the Duchess's hair and dirt on her clothing.

"I'll be back to change for dinner," Jax said, waving goodbye as she left her chambers in a whirlwind.

Perry was waiting outside of her door, looking restless. "Your grandfather's carriage just pulled up. Crepsta is here, too."

"Oh, Grand-Père will not like that." Jax couldn't resist a light chuckle. Duke Mensina was not fond of sharing the spotlight with anyone.

"Luckily, Jaquobie knows that. He's already shown Duke Crepsta and his wife to their chambers. He said you'll greet them at a private reception in just a bit."

Rolling her eyes, she cringed. As politically correct as Jaquobie's actions had been, she did not want to be forced to spend time alone with Duke Crepsta.

"We'll head over together after greeting your grandfather,"

Perry said, as if reading her mind.

"Thank you," she whispered softly, sharing a secret smile as her guardsmen followed them toward the entrance hall.

†

Creaking open to herald in their latest arrival, the grand doors of the castle had barely parted before Duke Mensina's imposing form marched inside.

"Jacqueline!" the Duke said in a booming voice, his burly arms spread wide to scoop up his granddaughter. "You look radiant. Being a bride suits you." He stroked her cheek with a fondness he never would have displayed up until recent years.

"Well, let's hope she's only a bride once," Perry chimed in with a sheepish chuckle.

Nodding heartily in acknowledgement, Duke Mensina turned his attention back to Jax, his dark violet eyes showing more signs of age since she'd last seen him.

"How are you, Grand-Père?" she asked, squeezing him in return.

"I can't complain. Your aunts send their love and their regrets that they couldn't make it. Adella is due with her fourth, or maybe her fifth child soon, and Adelaide is in charge with overseeing the duchy while I'm gone," he said, referring to the twin sisters who were a few years younger than Annette. "Young Amia is spending the spring in Zaltor, learning more about the Ancient Faith from the high priestesses."

Jax frowned. Zaltor was the only nation in the realm whose residents still widely followed the doctrine of the Ancient Faith. While it was tolerated and allowed within the borders of most duchies, it was rare to find large groups practicing the faith anywhere but Zaltor. "What in the name of the Virtues is she doing there?"

The Duke puffed out his chest, not looking happy. "Well, I've been working on a trade agreement with Duchess Zaltor regarding clay export for a new observatory I want to build. She's agreed, of course, but we're mining the clay from a few parcels of land that Ancient Faith temples reside on. Amia's gone just to keep things civil while the project is underway."

76

Jax nodded, understanding the need for diplomacy. "Well, I'm sad my dear aunts won't be able to join in the celebrations, but it sounds like things are progressing well for Mensina."

"Indeed," the Duke said with a gruff nod. "Am I correct in stating that Annette and Darian have already arrived?"

"Yes, they got in yesterday. They both look well."

He did not look reassured. "Be that as it may, I'm concerned about implementing taxes so soon after Cetachi has been stabilized."

"As am I, but I believe I have a solution." Even though she had promised herself not to discuss state business during the wedding, she quickly disclosed her tariff proposal to her grandfather.

He beamed as she finished. "Bright girl, Jacqueline. I'll expect the agreement on my desk by the time I arrive back home."

No rest for the weary, she thought. "Please, Grand-Père, let me show you to your suite. You must be tired from the journey." With that, she laced her arm through his and led him to a magnificent apartment in the eastern wing.

"Annette is just down the hall. We shall speak more at dinner," she said with a kiss on the cheek, dismissing herself. She didn't want to keep Duke Crepsta waiting any longer, and she could tell her grandfather was eager to see his daughter for the first time in six months.

As she and Perry walked to their next engagement, Hendrie appeared in the shadows. "Duchess," he whispered, although they were alone in the halls, aside from Jax's assigned sentries, "the boy has woken up."

Jax shot a desperate look at Perry, her heart torn. She needed to speak with the lad to figure out what had happened to Uma, but she also had her ceremonial duties to attend to. "Hendrie, ride out to find George and bring him to Master Vyanti's chambers as soon as possible. He's likely still investigating the remains of Uma's carriage. We'll give the boy a few minutes to sort out his thoughts then be down."

Saluting his orders, Hendrie disappeared just as silently as he had arrived.

"Let's keep this visit short," Jax grumbled, pulling Perry along to Duke Crepsta's quarters.

Just as she had envisioned, the small gathering began on a tense and awkward note. Ever since the Duke's nephew had been involved in a plot to overthrow Jax and take Saphire for his own, Crepsta's relationship with Saphire had been strained, to say the least. She had to give the old man credit for the effort he was making, and she managed to have a pleasant conversation with his wife about her wedding cake.

Perry, ever the charmer, was her knight in shining armor. "Duke Crepsta, Jacqueline tells me you bestowed a Crepstian stallion to her for her eighteenth birthday. I've seen the creature. He is a sight to behold."

Particularly proud of their noble steeds, valued throughout the realm for their swiftness and strength, the Duke launched into a tale about his first time riding one of the fabled mounts, supplying the conversation for the reminder of the brief reception.

"We are delighted you could be here to celebrate with us," Jax said with a gushing smile as she signaled to Perry it was time to depart. "Our home is yours during your stay."

"We shall see you at dinner, Jacqueline," the Duchess replied. "I am looking forward to assessing your pastry chef's abilities." She patted her round middle.

"That wasn't too bad, now, was it?" Perry asked once they were out of earshot and on their way to Vyanti's room.

"No, but thank goodness you were there. All I could think of to talk about was what an arse of a nephew he had," Jax muttered.

Before she could push open the door to Vyanti's chambers, Perry drew her back. "Shouldn't we wait for George?"

Jax folded her arms, her nostrils flaring. "It could be an hour before he's back. I don't feel like waiting."

"Luckily for you, that won't be necessary." George appeared at the top of the stairs leading down to the lower corridor, Hendrie at his side.

"He arrived just as I was tacking up my horse," Hendrie explained.

"My men are securing the fireblooms as we speak, and we'll bring the bodies of the two guards down, away from prying eyes," George said, responding to Jax's unasked questions. "The boy is awake?"

Nodding, Jax pushed open the door and barged into the dark chamber. "Vyanti?" she called out, wary of the lone flickering candle casting shadows on the walls.

"Shhhh!" the old man's voice hissed from the darkness. "I'm afraid Bastion is concussed, so I'm trying not to tax his senses too much."

"Bastion?"

Materializing before them, Vyanti picked up the candle holder, bringing it closer to illuminate his wrinkled features. "The boy's name. He works at the flower shop in town and was assisting Uma with transporting the fireblooms back to the castle."

"Has he said anything else? Anything about the attack?" Jax asked with eagerness, careful to keep her voice low.

Vyanti shook his head. "He woke up confused as to where he was and how he got here. I figured I'd wait until you got here to do any real prodding." He motioned for the group to follow him to the bed in the corner.

The candlelight made it hard for Jax to see Bastion's face, but she could see his small chest rising and falling with more strength than when she'd first seen him.

"Bastion, the Duchess of Saphire is here to pay you a visit. She and her companions were the ones to find you," Master Vyanti said in a soothing voice. If Jax hadn't been fueled by fear for Uma, she would have been lulled to sleep by it.

"The Duchess?" a youthful voice responded, laced with a mixture of awe and confusion. "What's happened to me?"

Jax perched on his bed, taking his trembling hand in hers. "Hello, Bastion. Welcome to my home. You are safe now and being well-cared for by the best healer in the realm." She paused, studying his bruises in the firelight. His eyes were still closed, and he occasionally winced in pain. "My friends and I are hoping you can tell us what happened. Do you remember anything before you were attacked?"

"No, Your Grace." Bastion sounded tearful. "I wasn't even meant to accompany Lady Uma to the palace, but there wasn't enough room in the carriage for all the fireblooms. I had to carry a crate back. It was pretty heavy, so I was a bit distracted the entire time. I don't remember what happened. One minute I was walking along the road, the next, I woke up here."

Jax bit her lip, trying to conceal her disappointment at the young man remembering so little. "Did Lady Uma say anything to you that seemed odd? Did the soldiers?"

"No, Your Grace. I'm pretty good at being invisible. Not many people want to speak to the hired help." His demeanor changed from tearful to glum. "I'm sorry I don't have anything more helpful to share."

She patted his arm. "I'm just glad you're all right. Perhaps with more rest, your memory of the attack will return." She rose and backed away from the bed, ushering her companions out into the hallway.

The brighter light shining from the flaming sconces revealed disappointed expressions all around. "I so hoped he had caught a glimpse of who attacked him," Jax said, voicing everyone else's thoughts.

"He just needs more time," Vyanti reassured her. "He suffered a serious blow to the back of his head."

George furrowed his brow. "This young man is the only witness to a crime against the Crown. If word gets out that he survived, he could be in serious danger if his attackers think he can identify them."

"It won't get out," Jax vowed. Her glare around the small circle swore everyone to secrecy. "For now, he's my personal guest. If anyone sees or asks about him, we'll just say he's here to keep watch over the fireblooms. I'm trusting him to your care, Vyanti."

"I'm doing all I can, Duchess," he replied with a dip of his chin.

"Well, what do we do while we're waiting for his memory to return?" Perry asked.

Jax pulled out the kidnapper's note from her dress pocket, as she did not feel it would be safe anywhere other than on her person. "We need to figure out whose seal this is." She jabbed her finger at the sword-and-serpent crest.

Perry looked at it over her shoulder. "If it's not signet of a noble house, what else could it be? I don't know of any bandits who would use something like this."

"What about the Shadow Brethren?" George ventured.

Once a guild of thieves and outlaws, the Shadow Brethren had grown over the decades into an established brotherhood of assassins for hire throughout the realm. Jax and her friends had a brush with the guild nearly two years ago when it had infiltrated Mensina and caused chaos at a tournament feast.

"I remember their seal. This is not it," Jax murmured as she traced the inky sword with her finger.

"But perhaps someone within the Brethren has seen this before. Perhaps it belongs to a rival group that we've not yet encountered," George suggested.

She raised an eyebrow. "Are you proposing we should enlist the help of a gang of thieves and murderers? Why, Captain, I didn't think you had it in you."

He scowled. "As much as I hate the idea, it could be fruitful."

"I thought the Shadow Brethren had been run out of Saphire," Perry interjected. "Where would we even find them?"

"They no longer have an outpost here, but that doesn't mean they've been eradicated from our borders." George's mouth set in a tight line. "Saphire boasts some of the most picturesque and high-valued land in the realm. With what the gold guild members make from their contracts, I'd be surprised if one or two of them didn't somehow own an acre or two here."

Jax felt her stomach tighten. "Even if that's the case, I'm sure they would have made such a purchase under an alias. How would we root them out?"

The Captain's face soured. "I have my ways, Duchess."

"How quickly can you make this happen? We're running out of time, George." Her eyes flashed. "Every minute Uma remains with these thugs, she's in greater danger."

"I'll send my spies out immediately, and I'll have a report ready for you first thing tomorrow morning," George promised.

"Tomorrow morning?" *A day before the rehearsal reception*, Jax thought. They had so little time before the realm discovered something was seriously amiss in the Saphire court. She had never felt more vulnerable.

"Tomorrow morning at the *latest*," George revised. "In the meantime, we should get you back upstairs to prepare for the evening's events."

Rubbing her temples, Jax felt her eyes watering. "How am I supposed to entertain everyone tonight?"

Perry took her hand and kissed it. "You've performed under stress many a time, Jax."

"But this is different. Uma is in danger!" She was almost on the verge of shrieking.

"And when we find her she will be mortified to learn all the distress she's caused you," Hendrie said, displaying a shy smile at the thought of Uma's humility.

His encouraging words gave Jax a spark of hope. "When we find her," she repeated.

Chapter Eight

"Do you not like my choice?" Vita asked, her olive skin paling in the mirror's reflection.

Jax shook away haunting thoughts of Uma, wherever she may be, and focused on the silvery ball gown. "No, it's lovely."

Vita pursed her lips in response. "Your expression says otherwise, Duquessa." She lowered her voice, even though they were alone in the royal chambers. "Is everything all right? You've been a ghost of yourself this past hour."

Jax twirled her skirts, the candlelight catching the shimmering material, painting enchanted silver flames on the walls. "Lots on my mind, that's all." She could tell her lady's maid did not believe her excuse but she wisely let the topic drop.

"It will be a wonder if you're be able to keep your eyes open come your wedding day. So many parties. You must be exhausted," Vita said as she busied herself putting away the makeup brushes and tidying up the vanity.

Jax yawned, weariness setting in for a few other reasons as well. "It does seem like a lot, doesn't it?"

Vita nodded. "I understand wanting your friends to arrive early, and even your grandfather. But I'm surprised that Duke Pettraud and Duke Crepsta are here. I thought Perry didn't even like his father."

Jax shot daggers at her loose tongue. "That is *not* to be repeated, do you hear me?" She paused, wanting to soften her tone. After all, Vita was still learning her place within the Saphire court. "They're here because they are Saphire's most steadfast allies and their presence at my side will strike a formidable chord when the remainder of the realm arrives over the next few days."

"Oh, a glorified power move, then?" Vita said with a chuckle.

Jax rolled her eyes at the woman's brazen, if inappropriate, attitude. "Sometimes I forget that you grew up in a noble house, you know that?"

Vita gave her a wicked grin. "I was always getting my father in trouble with my big mouth. I think he's hoping that you'll whip me into shape."

"Yet another insurmountable task to add to my plate," Jax remarked, but spiraled into giggles at Vita's shocked expression. "You'd better learn to take it as good as you give it, dear."

"No wonder Uma was so desperate to leave this post." As Vita moved to leave the room, she turned back around to face Jax. "Where is she, by the way? She and I made plans to figure out what jewels you should wear to the rehearsal reception, and she never showed."

Even as her insides crumbled, Jax maintained a calm façade. "She's been flitting around like a newborn sparrow. It's been so hard to keep track of her with everything going on. I'm sure she'll…be by soon." Jax struggled to lie to her maid's face. "But I'd actually like to choose my own jewelry, so why don't we do that sometime tomorrow, yes?"

"Of course, Duquessa," Vita said with a prim curtsy, then left the room.

Fanning herself to calm her nerves, Jax realized she needed to come up with a better excuse than that for tonight's dinner. Uma's absence would no doubt be noticed by her guests.

A knock on the outer chamber door interrupted her thoughts, and George stepped hesitantly into the room.

"Any news about the Shadow Brethren?" she asked, breathless with anticipation.

He shook his head. "No. Apologies, Jax, but that's not why I'm here. I figured I would personally escort you to the banquet hall. It might raise too many questions if people noticed you walking the corridors with heightened security."

"You're probably right. I'm sure there are already whisperings about it considering how I paraded around with them earlier." Jax detested how quickly gossip traveled within the walls of a palace.

George's shifting stance told her that this was indeed true. "I overheard Duke Crepsta sharing his concern with Perry's father earlier that he thought the increased security was an affront to *his* duchy and wonders if you truly believe Crepsta to be an ally."

Jax's upper lip curled. "You'd think that after all that transpired between his nephew and Saphire, he'd give us a little slack."

"Luckily, your grandfather was in the room and came to the rescue. He said it was likely a training exercise for the guards to prepare them for when the real threats arrive." George frowned. "It doesn't paint my men or me in the most capable of light, but it did the trick."

Jax placed a hand on his armored chest. "I thank your ego for taking the hit on my behalf."

He held the door open for her and led the way to the banquet hall. "Have you given any thought how you're going to address Uma's absence tonight?"

Jax paled. "I've been racking my mind, but the best I can come up with is that she's taken ill."

"That will make it seem as though she's not strong enough to see this through," he replied, poking a hole in her idea.

"I know, and with all the scrutiny she's bound to be under for being common-born, I'd hate to tarnish her reputation when the circumstances are completely my fault."

Stopping abruptly, George turned to face her, his eyes blazing. "This isn't your fault, Jax. You need to stop blaming yourself. Uma knew what she was getting into when she accepted the position. Hell, if anyone is to blame, it's me. I should have been aware there was a threat to your throne."

Jax could see from his forlorn expression that the guilt had been eating away at him. "How could you have known? I read the same reports as you do, George. Every morning. There has been nothing to indicate any type of plot or uprising."

He suddenly seemed a decade older than his thirty-seven years.

"I just feel that I've failed this duchy one too many times."

Knowing he referred to the murder of her parents, she grasped his arm. "You are my oldest friend and the only man I truly trust besides Perry." *Perhaps even more so*, she shamefully admitted. "You have not failed me in all our years together. Regardless of the actions of others, you have been true. Do not forget that."

He broke away from her gaze and bowed his head for a moment, clearly overcome by her words. "Thank you, Your Grace. I needed to hear that."

"And my guests need to see me. Let's go," she said, navigating away from the unpleasant topic.

He resumed his march, leading the way, and within minutes, Jax heard her name ringing out through the banquet room, announcing her arrival.

Perry was already seated in his usual chair, his father beside him. Having instructed the stewards beforehand, Jax made sure Duke Crepsta was seated to her right to make him feel as welcome as she could. In Uma's absence, Hendrie had taken over, checking that everyone was in their assigned place, skillfully covering up Uma's empty chair by sitting in it himself.

As she glided across the room, Jax could tell she was going to be in for a long evening. Perry's brothers were seated on either side of their father and Duke Crepsta's wife, which meant that aside from Perry, her closest friends and family were four chairs away, an unsuitable distance for conversation.

Charles gave her a slight wave as she walked by, nodding his head in the direction of his clearly smitten sister and Lady Carriena, each of whom were in fawning discussion with their male companions. She managed to mask her laughter, but she could see from the sparkle in Charles's eyes that he knew he had tickled her.

Arriving at the head of the table, looking out at the sea of faces greeting her, Jax once again wondered if someone among their party had a hand in Uma's disappearance. The Shadow Brethren were hired assassins. Who was to say Uma's kidnappers weren't for hire themselves?

Clearing her throat in preparation to speak, she gazed serenely at the faces of her newest guests. "Greetings, my dear friends from

Pettraud, Crepsta, and Mensina. While I am proud to call Duke Mensina family, I am honored that soon the same will be said about Duke Pettraud." She stopped to raise her golden goblet, first toward her grandfather, then her future father-in-law. "Saphire holds its friends dear and seeks to protect them with all her strength," she said, her eyes sliding to Duke Crepsta. She saw him blush under his peppery beard. "May we celebrate that bond these next few days." She lifted the glass to her lips, taking a deep, refreshing sip.

"Long live Duchess Jacqueline!" Her grandfather led the chorus with gusto.

Settling down to her plate, Jax prayed that no one would ask about Uma, and it was not until the main course of pork tenderloin arrived that Philippe, after surveying the table, cleared his throat.

"Your Grace, I had hoped to meet your new lady-in-waiting. She wasn't around when we were received this morning. Frankly, I'm beginning to wonder whether she actually exists." He clutched his napkin in his hand, assessing her reaction with a snide stare.

Jax smiled, although it did not reach her eyes. "Without her, this dinner wouldn't be happening, dear Philippe. Uma has been effortlessly managing the wedding preparations. I demanded she take the evening off and rest. She, of course, wouldn't hear of it, but considering it was a direct order from me," Jax paused, hoping her false bravado was working, "she complied."

A bemused smirk slid across the eldest Pettraud brother's face. "My, my. I guess I'll have to wait a bit longer before seeing if a commoner can really do the work of a nobleman."

"Really? You need proof?" Darian's voice raised in challenge, despite his being several seats down the table.

"I meant no offense, Sir Fangard." Philippe's apology rang false.

Darian's expression turned steely. "It's *Duke* Fangard, if you please."

Jax jumped in to deescalate the tensions. "Yes, Philippe, I ask that you show the Duke the respect he deserves. After all, Cetachi is a valued friend of Saphire." She watched with narrowed eyes as the arrogant man bristled at her reprimand.

Duke Pettraud coughed loudly, but the distraction did not deter Jax from noticing that he kicked his son under the table.

Cringing, Philippe straightened in his seat. "Apologies, Duchess."

She noted that he did not extend the same courtesy to Darian.

Perry shifted in his seat, his cheeks burning at his older brother's lack of decorum. She couldn't help but remember Perry's boyishly improper behavior when he first arrived in Saphire and how little restraint he'd used with his own words. But he was never cruel, even then, as his brother now appeared to be.

The hush that followed deafened the room. Jax took it upon herself to use the quietness to her advantage and engage in conversation with her friends seated farther away. "Lady Carriena, Viscount Emyr? Did you enjoy your ride on the grounds today?"

Always one to revel in the attention of a room, Carriena eagerly filled the silence. "Indeed. We traveled quite some distance, did we not?" She looked to Emyr and Bran for confirmation. "All the way to Lake Saltrine, I believe. Although," her brows drew together, "I will be the first to admit I did get a little lost along the way. Luckily, the good Baron here found me," she said with a nod to Skander.

Jax's eyes darted between Bran and Emyr. What had commanded their attention to the point they hadn't noticed Carriena was missing? The presence of an attractive woman such as herself would have been hard to forget when in their company.

"Did she give us an earful for taking off without her, or what?" Emyr chuckled, sharing a joke with his brother.

"You must have been preoccupied with something truly extraordinary to leave my friend behind." Jax hoped she sounded light and teasing as she pressed for more information. It occurred to her that the Viscounts had been away from the castle around the same time as the attack on Uma's carriage.

From the corner of her eye, she saw Perry's face go pale, as if he had had the same thought.

"The scenery was just that distracting, I guess," Emyr replied, the corners of his mouth turning up ever so slightly.

Unsatisfied with the answer, Jax tried not to look too dismayed. She didn't want to raise suspicions of anything being amiss.

The room slowly filled with chatter, Philippe's outburst forgotten by everyone except Jax, and perhaps Darian, by the time dessert arrived.

Duchess Crepsta moaned with delight as she tasted the flambéed peach tarte. "Oh, Jacqueline! My compliments to the chef."

Jaquobie spoke up from his chair a few seats down. "Her Grace's executive chef has studied with the masters in Savant."

That seemed to impress the squat woman. "My dear, we must send ours to learn some of these dishes," she said to her husband.

The exchange brought a genuine smile to Jax's lips. It was her great-grandfather who had taught her father that a world-class chef was the best delegate to conduct diplomatic relations, hence the reason the late Duke Saphire had ensured the highest quality kitchen staff.

The sommeliers were more conservative with the frequency in which the wine was poured this evening, for which Jax was grateful. She didn't have it in her tonight to go along with the drunken shenanigans of her guests, and she was relieved when everyone said good night at dinner and departed with their courtiers leading the way to their suites.

Jax and Perry stood together at the door, bidding their guests good night as everyone sauntered off.

"Apologies once again on behalf of my son, Duchess," Perry's father offered when he stood opposite them, the last in line. His lavender eyes watched the shadows disappear down the hallway before turning to Jax to say more. "I worry about that elitist behavior of his. I don't know where it comes from. My wife was so diligent in her quest to instill good values in him."

From his wistful tone, Jax wondered if the Duke had doubts about his oldest son becoming a wise ruler. Philippe's display so far had left her unimpressed.

Beside her, Perry stiffened at the mention of his mother, who had died a few months before Jax's own parents.

Knowing she would have to mediate this sensitive conversation, Jax chose her words with care. "Perry has told me many wonderful things about your wife. I know my parents were very fond of her."

"Your father and I often joked that Penelope and your mother's bond was the only reason he and I were friends." He looked incredibly sad at the memory of his late wife. "I wonder if I've done her a grave disservice, considering how the boys have turned out." He cast a look at Perry, and Jax took his arm in a show of support, fearing Duke Pettraud was about to say something crushing. "Not you, though, Percival. Despite the odds against you that were created by your brothers and, I suppose, myself, you have turned into a fine young man. You've done more for your duchy than all your brothers combined."

Perry's mouth dropped open, speechless. Jax, too, felt her heart beating so wildly she thought the Duke might be able to hear it.

I guess the sommeliers were a little more covert with their wine pouring than I thought, Jax surmised, for it seemed too much mead could be the only possible reason for this loose-lipped admission.

"Well, good night, you two." The Duke clasped his hands behind his back and strode away, following his assigned courtier.

"Did that just happen, or am I hallucinating?" Perry said, breaking the stunned silence between them once they were alone.

Jax broke into a grin. "I believe that just happened, Percival."

Perry laughed while shaking his head in disbelief. "'A fine young man'. *My* father called *me* a fine young man."

Jax linked her arm through his. "Why are you surprised? Are you not a fine young man? That's who I thought I was marrying."

He ignored her teasing, still shaking his head. "I can't believe it," he said in a whisper.

Jax thought he might have been speaking more to himself than to her. As Perry took time to process his father's elusive praise, she reflected on the conversation as well. Duke Pettraud's criticism of Philippe troubled her more than she cared to admit. This was his duchy's future leader, one of her strongest allies. She couldn't imagine cooperating with anyone who behaved daily the way Philippe had at dinner. She initially thought it was a one-off outburst, but the Duke's words made her think this was Philippe's normal attitude. And what about Perry's other brothers? What were they up to that made the Duke believe his wife would be upset by how they turned out?

From Perry, she knew them to be bullies but that was back during their childhood years. Surely by now they had grown out of tormenting people. She didn't know a thing about their work within the dukedom, and the more she thought about it, the more worried she grew. Long ago, she thought her marriage to Perry was all that was needed to ensure a continued ally in Pettraud, but once the mantle passed on to Philippe…she wasn't sure she wanted someone like him standing at her side in the political arena.

"I feel like our thoughts are going in opposite directions," Perry said, interrupting her swirling ideas. "You don't look pleased."

"I am happy for you, of course," she said, giving his arm a tender pat, "but I'd be lying if I said your father's words didn't have me worried."

"You're concerned about Philippe?"

"Aren't you?" Jax countered. "You know him better than I, Perry. Does he really have it in him to govern his people with a just and fair hand?"

His eyes darkened. "Of course not. But that's because my feelings toward him are more than a little jaded."

"I don't think you should be so quick to dismiss those feelings, my love. You have seen his true self."

He snorted. "I have, and he's an ugly beast, that is certain. But what can we do about it?"

In an ideal world, Jax knew exactly what she would do: seat someone else on the throne. But unfortunately, that was not how succession worked in the realm…*yet.* "We must be careful, for now. But this is something we will need to reconsider at a later time."

"You mean, once my father either steps down or dies?"

She gave him a sharp look for being so crude. "Let's be honest. Your father is never going to step down."

Perry conceded with a shrug. "True."

As forthcoming as she had been with her thoughts about Philippe, Jax decided to keep one thing to herself. It was obvious that the eldest Pettraud heir had some pent-up resentment over Darian and Uma's ascension to power. As images of the overturned carriage flashed in her mind, she wondered if he had decided to act on it.

Chapter Nine

"A pleasant evening, Duquessa?" Vita asked as she entered the Duchess's chambers to ready her for bed.

Narrowing her amethyst eyes, Jax assessed Vita's grim expression. "Why do I feel like you already know how it went?"

Fluffing a pillow, Vita paused before answering. "The kitchens were bustling about Lord Philippe's comments when I was down there collecting my supper." Pulling back the bedsheets with care, she continued. "I've never known a household that has more respect for its mistress than yours, Jacqueline. All anyone could talk about was how impressed they were with how you handled the matter and stood up for Duke Fangard."

"Philippe's behavior was brutish and uncalled for. I would never let anyone speak that way to guests at my table…or anyone, for that matter."

"He does sound like a cad."

Jax met her maid's remark with a grunt. "You can say that again."

"Well, let's hope you don't have to go out of your way tomorrow to entertain him."

Jax stood still as Vita went to work unlacing her gown. "Fortunately, I have other matters to attend to than Lord Philippe's entertainment needs."

"I thought you had put all matters of state to rest for the weekend," Vita commented as she slid Jax's nightdress over her head. "What are you working on now?"

Jax bit her tongue. "I just meant there are other guests here that I'll be devoting my time to."

"I saw the Viscounts of Carwyn earlier today while I was walking through the castle. I didn't realize they would be here."

"Do you know them?" Jax asked, surprised that Vita knew of the brothers.

"Oh yes," she replied with a nod. "They used to frequent my father's vineyard in their youth. Rumor has it that their father, the Marquess, shipped them off to Savant regularly because they caused so much trouble at home."

"Really?" Jax's curiosity was piqued; Perry had failed to mention this to her. "Do you know what kind of trouble they got themselves into?"

Vita bit her lip. "I'm not one to spread vicious gossip, especially since this all happened when they were much younger."

"Says the girl who gossiped to me about the gossip in the kitchens," Jax countered with a knowing smirk.

Blush crept from Vita's cheeks to her neck as she tucked her unruly dark hair behind her ear. "Well, Duquessa, it was rumored that the Viscounts participated in a gambling circuit run by some unsavory characters."

While Jax did not gamble herself, she found it hard to believe that the brothers would be reprimanded for the vice. "What do you mean 'unsavory characters'?"

"The group was led by members of the Shadow Brethren."

Jax sucked in a breath. The Carwyn brothers had ties to the Shadow Brethren?

"What's more," Vita continued, wringing her hands, "is that the nature of the gambling was quite vulgar. Bets were taken against whether or not a commoner could survive a fight with a wild animal. Quite a few people died before the ring was disbanded."

"How horrible!" Jax winced at the inhumanity. "No wonder they were punished." She couldn't believe she was playing the doting hostess to such brutes. Did Perry know about his friends' shady pasts?

"Again, this was over a decade ago, and since then, the brothers have paid full restitution from their own inheritance to the families who lost loved ones in the fighting, something they, themselves, insisted upon doing to repent," Vita explained.

"What happened to the Shadow Brethren who were involved?"

Vita rubbed her chin in thought. "I believe most were apprehended and hanged for their crimes. I remember hearing that only one managed to elude capture, but I don't know what happened to him." She turned to the door to take her leave for the night. "My father tries to keep informed about the guild, so as not to sell wine to the wrong patron, if you know what I mean."

"Do you happen to know if there are any other criminal factions in the realm, Vita?" Jax asked. Perhaps Vita knew who was behind the sword-and-serpent crest.

She tossed back her dark hair with a laugh. "Another criminal organization dare compete with the Brethren? Good Virtues, no."

Jax sank onto her mattress, her hopes dashed. "Stimulating conversation, as ever, Vita. Good night."

"Good night, Duquessa," she replied with a curtsy and left the room.

Lying her head back on the dove-feather pillow, Jax examined the silky canopy above her, searching for answers that were not there. Her doubts surrounding her guests began to multiply. She had Philippe with his grudge against commoners, Carriena and her father's financial woes, and now the Viscounts and their ties to the Brethren. What if the Viscounts only appeared to sever ties with the organization? Could they be behind Uma's disappearance? With dread, she recalled that Bran and Emyr had been off riding unsupervised around the time the carriage was attacked. First thing in the morning, she would ask Jaquobie to mandate that courtiers accompany all guests during their leisure activities and not just act as their escorts to and from areas of the palace. With this new threat, she didn't want to take any chances that something might slip past their watch.

‡

A knock on the door jolted her from sleep. Fumbling with her nightstand, Jax managed to light a candle, banishing the shadows of night. Tiptoeing to the door, she cracked it open a sliver.

George's chocolate eyes shimmered in the dim light. "I'm sorry to wake you, Jax, but I knew you'd want to hear this."

"What time is it?" she mumbled, rubbing sleep from her eyes as she waved him into the sitting room.

"Just past two. My spies have returned with some information regarding the Shadow Brethren's presence in Saphire."

Fully awake at the mention of the guild, she sat in her chair, inching forward. "And?"

"There appears to be a member of the Brethren on holiday here, renting a cottage down by the Saltrine."

"On holiday?" she repeated. "You've got to be joking."

"I guess even criminals need a break from the daily grind," George answered with a wry smile. "But what's more important is that this man has agreed to speak with me in exchange for immunity."

"Speak to *us*, you mean," Jax corrected, and before George could protest, she added, "I don't like the idea of bargaining with thugs."

"Neither do I." He leaned forward in his seat and took her hands. "But I'm not sure we have much choice if we're looking to resolve this matter quickly before something worse happens."

"Something worse than our men being attacked, and Uma kidnapped?" Jax stared at the pile of charcoal in the unlit fireplace. "No, I guess we don't," she said simply, turning to meet her friend's stare. "Can you arrange for a meeting?"

George nodded. "We can head out first thing in the morning, if you'd like?"

"Yes, the sooner the better." She nodded, pleased at his efficient work. "I will have Perry greet guests on my behalf in case anyone arrives while we are away. I also need to speak to Jaquobie about our courtiers."

Worry haunted George's eyes. "Why? Are they not doing a good job?"

Jax stood and made her way to the doorway of her bedroom. "I know they are like shadows within the castle walls, but it seems they did not accompany Carriena, the Baron, and the Viscounts during their ride today."

George's bushy eyebrows rose. "You think they were up to something?"

Jax brought him up to speed on the intriguing information Vita had shared with her about the brothers' history.

"That *is* troubling. It's very plausible that they still have connections to the guild and its dirty work." George paused, then thoughtfully stroked his chin. "You've never heard Perry mention any of this?"

"No. I can only assume that this all happened before they were acquaintances." Seeing the Captain's frown, she faltered for a beat. "What's that look supposed to mean?"

George simply stared at her.

Realization hit Jax like a thunderbolt. "You think Perry is *in* on this?" It was all she could do to keep from shrieking.

"I think *everyone* is a suspect until cleared," he slowly replied. "I just find it hard to believe that Perry doesn't know about his friends' pasts. He could very well be purposefully keeping the information from you."

Jax stomped her foot. "Why in the name of the Virtues would Perry do that?"

"I don't know, Your Grace."

"Clearly, you have an idea." She continued to press when he would not meet her fierce glare. "Go on, tell me."

"It's my job to think of all possible threats against the throne. It's nothing personal, Jax."

She folded her arms across her heaving chest. "It *is* personal when you accuse my fiancé of keeping secrets from me."

George cleared his throat. "The idea did occur to me that Perry could be aware of the Viscounts' connections to the Shadow Brethren and has been using that to his advantage."

"How does kidnapping Uma work in his favor?" Jax asked, reeling from the allegations assaulting her ears.

"Well, if the Shadow Brethren ends up being implicated in her attack, resentment for the group would spread like wildfire. Your people adore Uma. They would want the guild hunted down and brought to justice. Only more so if something else were to happen…say, to their Duchess." The words tumbled out of George's mouth like bile. "If it came to that, Perry could very well slip into your vacant throne, promising retribution for your death."

Jax sank to the floor, hardly believing what she was hearing from her friend. "You think that Perry's ultimate goal is to have me killed and take the throne for himself?" Her lips parted in utter amazement. "Are you *insane*?"

"I know it sounds farfetched, Jax—"

"It sounds preposterous, George!" she roared, no longer bothering to control her temper. "This is *Perry* we're talking about."

"Would you have once said the same thing about Aranelda?" he challenged.

Jax was dangerously close to slapping him across the face for his insolence. "That was uncalled for, Captain," she hissed, but his words had hit their target. Once, Aranelda had been like a sister to her, and Jax had trusted her above all else. Yet, she had been deceived and betrayed by the woman in the cruelest way.

George's face was a well of regret. "I'm sorry, Jax, but you have to understand my concerns."

"I'll ask Perry about Emyr and Bran's past and see what he says," she decided, reeling in her anger. "I'll meet you at the stables at dawn." She didn't bother saying good night. Her rage was still too near the surface to be entirely civil. How could George believe that her future husband could be behind something so sinister? She punched a pillow in anger.

Good luck getting any sleep now, Duchess, she thought irritably, looking out the window to her balcony. She scowled as the stars winked back.

Chapter Ten

"A bit early for breakfast, my love," Perry murmured after opening the door to his private suite. His curls were a tangled mess, indicating her knocking had summoned him from his pillow.

"I'm not here for breakfast." She marched into the room, her mind a battlefield of guilt and doubt. "Perry, I must ask you something."

"Go on," he said slowly, his eyebrows arched in confusion at her curt tone.

"When did you befriend Emyr and Bran?"

Whatever tension had been building inside him seemed to dissipate. "What a random question, Jax. You had me worried there for a moment." He stroked the stubble on his chin. "I guess Father arranged for the introduction several years ago."

Jax forced herself to continue. "Why?"

"Well, I think Father wanted the Marquess to start paying more in taxes, and he thought a friendship between their sons might soften him up."

"Why would the Marquess agree to such a thing?"

"Please, Jax." Perry gave her an annoyed frown. "Despite my being the youngest in House Pettraud, I still am a member of the royal family, and it would be considered an honor to be in my confidence."

"That was the only benefit to the Marquess?" Jax pressed.

"Well..." Perry said, scratching his head, "I guess I do remember my mother being the one to tell me that the Marquess was hoping I could be a good influence on his sons. I guess they were quite wild as teens, and...well, I was not."

He can't possibly be this good at appearing clueless, can he? Jax asked herself as her resolve began to waiver. "Do you know what was meant by 'wild'?"

"Where is all this going, Jax?"

"Just answer the question, Perry." Tears welled up in her eyes. "Please."

Clearly troubled by her reaction, he searched for an answer. "Well, I don't know. It never came up. They seemed like gentlemen to me by the time we were finally introduced. A bit boisterous at times, but nothing that ever gravely concerned me."

Was that truth in his eyes? She hated herself for doubting the man before her.

"Jax, something is wrong." Perry stepped closer until he was at her side. "What is it?"

"Oh, Perry." She couldn't hold the tears of fear back any longer and buried her head into his nightshirt. "I'm so sorry. I'm an awful person."

"What? What's this about? Has something happened to Uma?" Perry gripped her by the arms. "Jax, tell me."

"Please don't be mad," she whispered as she tasted salt on her lips. "It's just that...we've learned some unsavory information about your friends..."

"Such as?"

Jax swallowed her emotions. "Apparently, in their youth, Emyr and Bran fell into business with the Shadow Brethren."

Perry's eyes looked like they might pop out of his head. "*What! Where did you hear such a thing?*"

"It doesn't matter where I heard it," Jax said, wishing to protect Vita. "What matters is that two of our royal guests have connections to the assassin's guild—"

"And you think they might have something to do with Uma's disappearance," Perry finished. He paced the length of his room as he processed the news. "I can't imagine either of them being involved. They're loons, mind you, but it's all in good fun."

"We can't be certain until we know more about their ties to the Brethren."

Perry stopped in his tracks. "Why were you so nervous to tell me this? They are my friends, yes, but surely you know you can talk to me about anything."

Jax's cheeks flushed as she broke away from his gaze. "I know that…"

He crumbled before her eyes. "You thought I already knew?" He sank into a nearby chair, burying his face in his hands.

"I'm so sorry, Perry."

The catch in her throat revealed more than she planned to. He looked up at her again, heartbreak written all over his features. "Did you think I was using them? That *I* was behind Uma's disappearance?"

"No!" Jax said, rushing forward. She fell to her knees before him. "No! I-I knew deep down that you couldn't do something so cruel to me, to our duchy."

"But the thought entered your mind, didn't it?" Perry snarled as he stood up and walked away, as if her touch disgusted him.

"No," she stammered again, "no, I couldn't believe it." She tried to rein in her gasping breath. "But Arnie…"

"I am *not* Aranelda." Perry's voice boomed, the windows shuddering at his thunder. His chest heaving, he came back to where she sobbed on the floor and knelt beside her. "I could never hurt you, Jax, and it pains me that you don't believe in our love enough to see that." He took both of her hands in his, her fingers covered in tears. "I know you've been through a great deal, but we can't go into our marriage not trusting each other."

She felt a rise of panic in her heart. "What are you saying?"

He hung his head. "I don't know. I love you so much, Jax. I sometimes wonder if that love has blinded me."

"Perry, please. I made a mistake. I got caught up in worrying about Uma, and then after speaking to George…"

"George? So it's the Captain of the Ducal Guard who has you thinking I'm some sort of criminal mastermind?" Perry abruptly dropped her hands.

"No, no. It's just that we were considering all angles." Jax felt like she was unraveling at her core. "I mean, Carriena is on my list of suspects, for Virtues sake."

If she had hoped that would help her argument, it didn't. "Carriena? Goodness, Jax, what do people have to do in order for you to actually trust them? I'd love to know. What's George done for you that none of us can seem to hold a candle to?"

If she didn't know better, Jax would have thought Perry was jealous. "I do trust her. I do trust *you*, Perry! That's why I'm here."

"What, I should be comforted by the fact my future wife is not afraid to speak to me without an envoy to protect her?" His temper once again boiled to the surface.

Jax buried her face in her palms. "No, that's not what I meant. I do trust you, Perry. I defended you to George. I couldn't believe he suggested that you might be behind this. That's why I'm here talking to you, my love, trying to figure all this out. I'm just so desperate to find Uma. Please…" she trailed off, her sobs overtaking her ability to speak.

She felt his strong arms encircle her as she sat there on the stone floor, crying like a frightened child.

"Shhh, shhh, it's all right." His warm breath caressed her ear, his lips barely touching her skin. "It's all right, Jax."

She pulled away to look at his face and her whimpering subsided.

"I forget sometimes that you and I are not ordinary people. While I know I am in your heart, I do have to contend with that of your duchy." Perry inhaled, closing his eyes briefly in contemplation. "There are moments when I wish you and I could live a simple life, without a care in the world." He raised his hand to stroke her face, pushing away strands of hair so that he could see her amethyst eyes. "But you are the Duchess of Saphire. It's who you were born to be, and I love you for who you are. And it will be my role as your husband to accept that there will be times when your love for the duchy comes before your love for me. And I will find a way to live with that, because I would do anything just to have a sliver of your heart be mine."

Touched by his humbling confession, she embraced him with fierce strength. "As Duchess, you may be right," she murmured into his curls, "but as Jax, you do have all my heart." She sealed her pledge with a kiss.

Chapter Eleven

"I'm still not a fan of this idea of you riding out to meet a criminal."

She wriggled out from Perry's tight grasp. "I'll be fine. I just need you to promise to keep up the ruse while we are gone."

Jax, Perry, George, and Hendrie had gathered outside the stables, watching the sun peek over the distant hills as they waited for the horses to be brought out by the stable master.

"I have my orders," Perry said in mock salute.

Jax folded her arms as she tapped her foot impatiently, staring at the bustling stalls. She wanted this little jaunt to be over and done with. "I've given Jaquobie his orders as well. Our guests won't have a minute of their day to themselves going forward."

"We shouldn't be gone long," George stated, giving Perry a sheepish look. Jax had asked him to apologize to Perry, and the Captain had obliged during their walk down through the gardens.

Perry had, of course, been a good sport about it, but she sensed the tension lingering in the air. All was not quite forgiven, yet.

"Keep her safe," he said now, directing a stern look at the Captain.

George raised a fist to his heart. "On my life."

The stable master arrived with Jax and George's horses, assisting the Duchess as she climbed into the saddle.

"If anyone asks where I am—" she began.

"I'll tell them you're enjoying some well-deserved pampering," Perry said, rolling his eyes. They'd only discussed this seven or eight times in the last hour. "I plan to keep everyone entertained with some outdoor lawn games. Your presence won't even be missed," he teased.

Kicking her horse into a canter, Jax stuck her tongue out in his direction as she and George rode away. They opted to take the woodland trail, rather than the road, to ensure their mission was kept secret. With the earthy terrain uneven and littered with gnarled roots, they kept their horses' speeds at a brisk trot as they traveled through the forest.

"Where exactly are we meeting this man?" Jax asked as she bounced up and down on Mortimer's back.

"There's a small clearing just north of the east Saltrine bathhouse," George explained.

Jax remembered stopping at the bathhouse during her childhood after a long day of playing and swimming in the lake. "That doesn't seem very private."

"It's early enough in the season that there won't be many people around," George called back to her as his mount led the way. "Besides, I wanted it to be outside so my men can have better visibility."

"Men?" Jax whipped her head around, not seeing anyone.

"I have a squadron of fifteen soldiers shadowing us, in case things do not go according to plan," he stated in a rather lighthearted manner that contrasted with the topic at hand.

"I thought we were supposed to come alone."

"If you think for a moment that I'm going to lead the Duchess of Saphire into a clearing to meet a criminal with only one man for protection, you better check your corset," he said with a devious snort. "I'd say it's too tight and cutting off the blood flow to your brain."

"Very funny," Jax drawled, nevertheless smiling at his crass joke. "Do you know anything about this fellow we're riding off to meet?"

"I'm afraid the name he used to rent the cottage was an alias, so I do not know his true identity."

"Then how do we know we're speaking to a member of the

Brethren?"

"He has its seal branded into his skin. My spies saw it on his arm while he was drinking at the lakeside pub."

Jax shivered, recalling the threatening mark shaped like an X. "What if that means he's been targeted by the organization?" In her previous encounter with the Shadow Brethren, she didn't remember the rogue having a tattoo.

"Guild members with brands are high-ranking leaders."

Jax's face contorted with disgust. "I can't believe we aren't going to run him through the moment we get the information we need."

"As much as I would personally like to do that, it would not be wise for us to be seen going back on our word," George cautioned. "There's no doubt in my mind that our new friend has sent word to the Shadow Brethren that we are asking questions. If we renege on our promise of immunity and the guild was to retaliate, it could spell trouble for the people of Saphire."

The last thing Jax wanted was to cause her people harm. "I'm just concerned that the Brethren will think we welcome criminals into our lands with open arms."

"I think your record of apprehending killers and bringing them to justice suggests otherwise, Your Grace."

She blushed at his praise and began to marvel the beautiful woodlands surrounding them. The spring weather had been kind to the area, allowing it to flourish, bright blooms peppering the trees they rode past.

✟

Nearly two hours later, they entered a grassy clearing, the morning sun illuminating the glossy glade. George raised his hand to halt their steps, and she suspected it was also a signal for his soldiers to get into position. She still had not spied them amongst the trees, and she hoped their unpleasant guest had not either.

She slid off Mortimer's back, dropping his reins to the ground. "Nice place for a picnic," she offered, trying to ease the tension fortifying around them.

George's glare silenced her. "I didn't argue when you demanded to come, but you must follow *my* orders for once, Duchess. Remember, let me do the talking."

Her mouth opened, then closed with a snap. He was right. She had willingly put herself in an extremely dangerous position, George even more so. Without her present, he would just have the Shadow Brethren to contend with. Now, he had to add her safety to his list of concerns. She voiced an obedient whisper. "Yes, Captain."

Through the thicket at the opposite end of the clearing, they tensed at the shattering of branches.

"Someone's coming," George declared, stepping between Jax and the direction of the noise.

"Could have figured that out myself, thanks," Jax mumbled, only to be reprimanded by his dark gaze. She inverted her lips. *Shutting my mouth for good now.*

With a dramatic flourish that, despite the circumstances, almost made her laugh out loud, the bushes before them parted and a broad man stepped into the glade, his arms outstretched.

His rather gaudy azure tunic adorned with gold accents seemed over-the-top, especially for a woodland stroll. He removed his feathery hat and dropped to a low bow, the sheath of his silver sword marring the ground as it dragged over the earth. Resuming his cavalier stance, he stroked his pointy black beard and gave Jax an inquisitive look. "I did not expect to be received by the Duchess herself."

George took a step forward, his hand resting on his sword. "Who are you? Please state your name."

Their informant raised an eyebrow. "Isn't it obvious, Captain?"

"Your name, sir," George said with a growl. "Your alias does you no good on immunity papers."

Clearing his throat, the man nodded his head. "I am called Signor Daephanté within the guild. That is the name I wish to be used on my papers."

"How do we know you are with the Brethren?" George asked.

Rolling up his right sleeve, Daephanté held out his tanned forearm. Jax cringed at the unsightly brand scarred into his skin.

"I joined the guild as a young boy after my parents were killed in a raid," he explained, as casually as if reporting sunny skies outside. "Well, it was more coercion than volunteering, but since I had no family left, the Brethren became my home."

Jax knew she wasn't supposed to speak, but she couldn't help herself. "You willingly lived beside the people who murdered your parents?"

"We don't all have the luxury of a large treasury to keep a roof over our heads, Duquessa." Daephanté's eyes raked over her, a crude smile growing large across his face.

Jax noticed George's jaw twitch with anger, and she knew it was directed at her for speaking out of turn.

"When did you receive the brand?" he asked, coolly ignoring her interference.

Daephanté mimed counting his fingers. "Let me think, let me think. I ascended to the inner circle not five summers ago."

George shifted his warrior stance. "And why are you here in Saphire? The guild's outposts have all been run out."

"Why, Saphire is beautiful this time of year. It's been a while since I've had the opportunity to take a trip."

The nonchalant way Daephanté answered the question made Jax tremble. This was an extremely dangerous man; he displayed not an ounce of fear in the presence of the Captain of the Ducal Guard.

"The timing seems curious," George replied.

Daephanté raised an eyebrow with regal poise. "Does it? Why's that?"

George looked like he was running out of patience. "It is common knowledge the Duchess is to be married in two days' time."

"Despite the fact my invitation seems to have gotten lost along the way, my sincerest congratulations, Duquessa," Daephanté said, accenting his words with a slight bow. "I wish you and your betrothed all the happiness in the world."

His words made her feel cold. She prayed to the Virtues that her marriage had not been tainted by his blessing.

"But alas," he continued, "it is merely a coincidence I am here. The Brethren does not dare operate within the borders of Saphire. We learned our lesson long ago, Captain." Daephanté stared off into the distance, seemingly lost in thought, before snapping his attention back to George. "Enough of these mundane questions. Let's get to the real reason you have summoned me here. I'd like to get back to reading my book by the lake."

George shot a quick look at Jax before proceeding. "Does the guild have any plans to sabotage the Duchess's wedding?"

Daephanté looked genuinely surprised by the question. "As I said, the Brethren does not dare operate within the borders of Saphire."

"A yes or no will do," George seethed.

The assassin's bronze eyes narrowed. "No, we do not."

George held a hand out to Jax. Digging into the pocket of her riding gown, she pulled out the threat left near the overturned carriage. "Have you ever seen this symbol before?" he asked, presenting the parchment to Daephanté.

His sun-kissed face visibly paled. "Where in the name of the Virtues did you find this?" he hissed.

"What does it mean?" Once more forgetting George's orders, Jax rushed forward, her eyes intent on the criminal. "Do you know who left this note?" Her heart pulsed in her anticipation.

Daephanté wrung his hands, his eyes darting around the clearing, as if searching for phantoms. "I-I do not know, Duquessa."

"Your reaction says otherwise," she said in a voice hard as stone. "What does this mark mean?"

He seemed to shrink before her as he stuttered a reply. "Th-there are rumors within the guild..."

"What rumors?" George demanded.

Daephanté looked from Jax to George, then settled his gaze on the Duchess. "Rumors of a dark threat growing in the realm. I-I—" he stammered, "I did not think they had traveled this far north."

"What kind of threat?" Jax asked, trying to keep calm and contain the fear roiling in her veins.

"A rebel faction, Duquessa. Last I heard, they were gathering supporters in Crepsta."

Jax and George exchanged wary looks. "Tell us what you know, sir," George said in a low growl, "or we shall force it from you."

Daephanté held up his hands in protest. "Please, I do not know much. The Brethren stays away from political matters."

"Except when you're hired to assassinate a leader," George

countered.

Daephanté's eyes widened at the accusation. "We have no interest in that arena anymore. We have scaled back our services, if you will. Eluding angry Ducal Guards is not worth the amount of gold anymore. We stick to easier contracts these days."

"So, this rebel faction is planning to assassinate a leader?" Jax asked, seizing the information he had let carelessly slip.

"Again, Your Grace, I do not know." Daephanté's face glistened with perspiration. "All that we have gathered is that this small group is on a personal vendetta. We know better than to get in their way."

Jax edged forward even more. "They're small in numbers?"

"Many believe their cause to be futile, and therefore don't want to risk being associated with such foolishness."

"I've heard enough," George said, abruptly grabbing Jax by the arm as he pulled her back to her horse. "We're getting you back to the palace now."

"What? Why?" Jax asked, struggling against his firm grip. She was no match for his strength.

"Did you not just hear the same information I did?" he said roughly. "A rogue faction has been gathering support to assassinate a leader. That same faction has kidnapped *your* lady-in-waiting."

Jax felt as if the ground had been dropped out from beneath her as the pieces clicked into place. "You believe *I* am their target?" Even as she spoke the words, she knew the answer.

"Signor Daephanté, your request for immunity has been granted, but I suggest you continue your holiday elsewhere. Tandora's coast is lovely this time of year," George called over his shoulder as he lifted himself onto his own mount.

Jax kicked Mortimer into action, closely trailing George as he rode out of the clearing. As soon as they burst from the thicket encircling the grove, a wall of Saphirian soldiers ascended on them, forming a protective barrier around her horse as they galloped away.

"Why kidnap Uma?" she puzzled aloud as they galloped back to the palace in tense silence. "Why not just kill her?" She thought back to the message on the note. *You have something of ours, so we took something of yours.* What did she have that this nameless band of rogues wanted? How could they hope to harm her when she was constantly surrounded by guards? She replayed Daephanté's words over and over in her head. He had been surprised that the faction was this far north, as he'd last heard they were gathering forces in Crepsta. Was the Duke aware of this rebellion growing within his own borders? Was he a part of it? Did he want to finish what his nephew had started?

She hardly noticed the changing scenery as they neared the palace and before long, she and George were dismounting behind the stables.

"You'll receive all your guests in the throne room today, Duchess...after they have been thoroughly searched by my men before entering the grounds." George's expression left no room for disagreement. Taking her by the arm, he led her through the maze of garden hedges.

She nearly stumbled trying to keep in step with his rushed pace. "George, please, slow down."

He didn't appear to hear her. "We should consider sending everyone home and postponing the wedding."

Her heart sank at the notion. Her marriage to Perry was the only thing keeping her from losing her mind from worrying about Uma. "We cannot send our guests away from the castle, George. We could be sending them right into a trap."

He shoved open a side door, pulling her into the confines of the palace. "I suppose you could be right." He hesitated a few seconds before adding, "I need to say this, so you can prepare yourself, Jax. We may not be able to rescue Uma if it risks your safety."

She felt her throat tighten, but she chose not to argue. Now was not the time.

If her silent acquiescence surprised him, he didn't show it. Instead, he pulled open the doors to the throne room and ushered her inside. "Stay here for now. I must meet with my security council about next steps."

She quickly decided against demanding to go with him. As much as she wanted to be a part of the strategic talks, it was not her forte. *And besides,* she thought as George closed the doors behind him, *if the Ducal Guard is unable to save Uma, I need to come up with a plan to do it myself.*

Chapter Twelve

After a few minutes of pacing the length of the throne room, Jax felt her stomach grumble. Their journey to the Saltrine and back had taken a good chunk of time, but since they'd left so early, she realized she could catch the end of breakfast in the banquet hall. It would also give her the chance to appease her guests, as she did not want them to catch wind of anything being wrong with her prolonged absence.

"I'd like to go to the dining room, please," Jax called out to her guardsmen, who stood across the enormous room.

"Your Grace, Captain Solomon's orders were for you to remain secure in this room," one of the armor-clad men responded.

"I cannot very well spend my entire day in here, sirs. The last time I checked, I outranked Captain Solomon, so the door, if you please." Her face was set hard as stone.

The guardsmen exchanged nervous looks before one moved to unlock the door. "We will escort you there, Your Grace."

Jax's hunger pangs triggered her temper. "Then let's get a move on."

She realized how ridiculous she looked, arriving at the banquet room with fifteen soldiers in her wake, but she breezed past all the questioning stares and made for her seat at the head of the table, despite all the surrounding chairs being empty. She had barely touched the cushion when a cherry tart was deposited on her plate by one of the dining room attendants.

"Good morning, everyone," she said with as much cheer as she could muster, hoping that she came off sounding relaxed and carefree. She looked down the length of the table, as everyone else had congregated near the opposite end. She was happy to see Charles, Darian, Annette, Giovanna, and Carriena waving back at her.

"We weren't expecting to see you so soon," Carriena commented, a smirk on her pretty face. "From Perry's description, it sounded like an entire bathhouse had been set up in your chambers."

Jax grinned through a mouthful of pastry. Just being here amongst friends made her feel at ease. "I guess I'm just not that good at putting my feet up. What have I missed?"

Charles's hand flew to his mouth to choke back a snort, eliciting a raised eyebrow from Jax. "Something entertaining, I take it?" she asked.

Carriena leaned an elbow on the table and sighed. "Oh, just a spat between the Pettraud brothers."

"Really?" Jax asked, intrigued. "What about?"

Giovanna's cheeks flushed, her eyes darting to Darian. "Lord Philippe was running his mouth about Cetachi again."

A grim Darian pointed to his brown eyes. "He called it a nation raised in dirt."

Before Jax could respond to the disgusting statement, Charles spoke. "Bet it will be the last time he says that, Duke. I'm surprised he woke up after that punch he took to the face."

"He was *punched*?" Jax dropped her fork. "In here?" A fistfight, in her dining hall?

Carriena laughed. "By Perry, of all people."

She wondered if she'd heard wrong. "Perry? Perry punched his oldest brother, the future Duke Pettraud, in my dining hall?"

Both Darian and Annette nodded, their grins replaced with more appropriate somber expressions.

"To make it even more unbelievable, Duchess, their father led *Philippe* away from the room by his ear," Giovanna offered. "It was quite a sight, seeing a grown man cower like that."

The cherry filling in her stomach turned to lead. "Where is

Perry?" she asked, placing her napkin down on the table with care.

"I believe his friends took him somewhere to cool off," Darian replied.

"After his father gave him a pat on the back," Annette mentioned with a meaningful look at Jax. She'd witnessed firsthand the strained relationship between Perry and the Duke at the peace summit last winter, so the Duke's action meant something.

Jax motioned to the guardsman closest to her. "Please send for Lord Pettraud," she ordered in a clipped tone.

Disappearing with a bow, the guard exited to complete his task.

"Anything else I should know?" Jax looked around the table.

Before her friends could reply, they were interrupted by Jaquobie rushing into the hall.

"Your Grace," he said with a bow, "I just received word that the delegation from Tandora has been held up due to a thrown horseshoe and will not be arriving until tomorrow."

Jax had to stop herself from looking relieved. One less thing to worry about for today, at least. "Thank you, Jaquobie. That just leaves the arrival of Carriena's father for today, yes?"

Her High Courtier tipped his chin. "Correct. The Duke plans to arrive before tonight's feast."

"So much eating," Carriena said with a sigh, rubbing her trim waist. "I'll need to adjust the size of my dresses by the time this wedding wraps up."

Lysette appeared at Jaquobie's side, looking lovely in a cerulean gown, and gave Jax a graceful curtsy before joining everyone at the table. "I went up a size within my first month of living here."

"And you look all the more stunning," Jaquobie said, kissing his wife tenderly on the cheek, a sight that still shocked Jax. "I shall return shortly. I've been summoned by Captain Solomon." Before leaving he cast an anxious glance at Jax.

No doubt George would fill Jaquobie in on all they had learned from Daephanté.

"Is everything all right, Duchess?" Giovanna's melodic voice cut through her thoughts. "You don't look as relaxed as I'd imagined you'd be after your morning."

Jax's grip on the arm of her chair tightened as she responded. "I suppose that even a clay bath cannot thwart the stress of the wedding."

"What's there to worry about?" Carriena said, popping a piece of muffin in her mouth. "Uma's handling everything, right? I don't think I've even seen the poor girl, she must be so busy."

Jax looked at her nearly empty plate, hating that she had to lie to her dearest friends. "Uma is working quite hard." She felt her friend's gaze bearing down on her. Carriena knew her better than just about anyone and would know doubt realize she was hiding something. "What have you all got planned for today?" Jax asked, changing the subject.

"I believe Perry has set up some games for us on the lawn. It is a beautiful day outside," Lysette said, casting a look up at the sunlight streaming in through the high stained-glass windows.

"I've heard rumors that he's quite adept with a quiver. I shall like to challenge him at that," Darian declared, puffing his chest out for Annette's benefit.

A side door creaked opened, the sound ringing throughout the vaulted ceilings. Jax turned, expecting to see Perry, but was surprised to find Master Vyanti escorting Bastion into the room.

Vyanti looked startled, then frightened, by all the curious faces staring at the pair, as if realizing he'd made a grave error by appearing in public. "Forgive me, Your Grace. I...we thought everyone would have departed by now, otherwise we would not have intruded."

"Nonsense," Carriena beckoned, stepping out of line in bold fashion. "The more the merrier."

Vyanti looked to Jax for confirmation before sitting down at the table with the young man. She nodded stiffly and motioned to the empty chairs surrounding her seat at the head of the table.

"Care to introduce us all, Jax?" Carriena asked, clearly curious as to who these latest visitors were.

"This is my court physician, Master Vyanti," Jax said, gesturing to the elderly man. "Charles, you mentioned wanting to meet the master. I'm sure you'll have plenty to speak about." She gave each a forced smile before turning her attention back to her food.

"And who is this young man?" Carriena prodded once more,

ever the thorn in one's side when she wanted to be.

"I'm the royal escort for the Duchess's flowers," Bastion chimed in, before stuffing a hardboiled egg in his large mouth in one bite. It only took him a few seconds to chew and swallow, and then he enthusiastically reached for another. "The florist sent me up here to take care of the arrangements."

"Oh," Carriena said dully, appearing to have lost interest after his first sentence.

Bastion slid a sheepish glance at Jax as she bowed her head, silently commending him for his authentic performance. He'd played his part well, knowing he might be in danger if word got out about why he was really at the palace.

When chattering at the opposite end of the table had resumed, Jax leaned in to speak with Bastion, keeping her voice low. "How is your head doing?"

"Much better, Your Grace," he answered, rubbing the spot for emphasis. To any observer, it would look like he was merely bashful in the presence of royalty. "It only twinges a bit now and then." He lowered his voice even more. "I'm afraid I still don't remember a thing. I was holding the fireblooms in my arms one moment, then the next, I woke up here."

Jax couldn't hide the disappointment in her eyes.

The opening of the main door signaled Perry's arrival. He marched into the room, his hands behind his back, his expression contrite. Apparently, her guardsman had seen to it that he was warned that she knew about his tiff with his brother.

"Good morning, dearest," she called, still sorting out her feelings about the incident. It didn't help that she was under scrutiny by her guests.

"Hello, Duchess," Perry answered, his eyes wary. "I trust your morning was peaceful?"

She recognized that he was fishing for information about the success of her meeting with the Brethren. "It was most illuminating," she replied, noticing how he visibly relaxed. "I hear breakfast was anything but."

His face darkened to a scowl as his eyes flew around the room, presumably searching for the guilty party who betrayed him. But he amazed her by keeping his mouth shut. At least he knew better than to rebuke her in public.

"I'm told various lawn games have been set up for our guests," she said in a brisk change of subject. "Shall we all head outside and seize the day?"

With that, she pushed her chair away from the table and glided to Perry's side, taking his arm. "It's a good thing I'm already dressed for sport," she commented, acknowledging that she still wore her riding outfit.

"Yes, you look like you've come straight from a spa," he sarcastically replied under his breath.

"It's been a little chaotic this morning. I forgot to pay attention to detail," she snapped as they led their friends out of the hall. She noticed her guards formed a protective layer around the group. She doubted George would be pleased at their allowing her to leave the castle, but she had other things to worry about.

Out of earshot from the others as they walked, Jax leaned in closer to Perry. "Care to explain how punching your brother seemed like a good idea?"

He growled beside her. "Jax, you should have heard the crude things he was muttering. Luckily, Darian only heard the comment about a nation of dirt. I couldn't stand for it."

"And hitting him was the solution?" Jax hissed.

"He's my brother. That's what brothers do."

Jax rubbed her temples. "It may be the case in normal circumstances, but brotherly love goes out the window when you're the future Prince Consort of one duchy and he's the future Duke of another!"

Perry snorted. "If anything, I think it helped our cause."

"What do you mean?"

"My father is furious with Philippe. In fact," Perry paused to make sure no one was nearby as they arrived at the lawn outside the garden, "I trailed the two of them back to their suites. Philippe was moaning about how dare I assault the future of Pettraud, and my father slapped him across the face."

Jax's eyebrows shot up. "Really?"

Perry nodded. "He said to my brother, and I quote: 'You're only the future of Pettraud if you make it to the throne alive'."

Jax exhaled long and low. "Well, that's not something I'd expect a Duke to tell his intended heir."

"I'm going to see if I can get more information from Kaul, but it seems like Philippe has been losing favor with Father, and not just during this visit." Perry paused for a moment. "I didn't tell you this at the time because I didn't think anything of it, but I was surprised that Philippe didn't attend the Lysandeir summit last winter with Father. Usually, he's the Duke's shadow at those types of things."

"It sounds like your father has been losing confidence in him for a while now." Jax crossed her arms as she looked out over the well-manicured lawn where all their friends had already begun to enjoy the activities provided. "I wonder if that means Philippe feels driven to commit desperate acts to secure his reign."

Perry waved off an invitation from Edmund and Skander to join in a game of croquette. He said to Jax, "What did you learn speaking with the Brethren member?"

Jax took a quick glance around before leading him to a small, gated alcove deep within the garden and away from their friends. Her guardsmen followed, silent and resolute. From there, she explained what she and George had learned from Signor Daephanté, watching Perry's expression grow more concerned.

"Jax, these rogues are obviously out to harm you. They declared their intentions by kidnapping Uma, and now just seem to be biding their time." He cast a worried glance around the inner sanctum of the garden. "I agree we can't send our friends into the hands of the enemy, but don't you think we should consider postponing the wedding?"

"For how long?" she pushed back. "Do we suspend our lives indefinitely until these brutes decide to make themselves known? I won't live my life in fear."

"But what about Uma?"

Jax felt a lump grow in her throat. "Deep down, I know she's still alive." Her eyes teared up. "But I can't figure out why they took her. And why they haven't sent a ransom demand for her safe return." She pulled the note out of her pocket and read its sinister scrawl once more, even though she'd memorized the threat by heart. "Part of their torture is making me wait. I don't know what I have that they want in return. Daephanté said it was a personal vendetta, not a political one."

"How are you even sure you can trust this man? What if he's just given you a false lead while the real plotting continues?"

Jax's face hardened. "Because if it turns out he is lying, his immunity and his life are forfeited. If there's one thing Shadow Brethren members value, it's their freedom."

Perry held her hands in his. "You know I want to marry you, Jax. More than anything. But how can we keep this charade up without Uma?"

"I spoke with the wedding planners yesterday. Uma was so well-prepared, she'd already made sure everything for the ceremony was in place before our guests even started to arrive." She stroked the lace of her riding gown. "The ladies will ensure everything is set up and executed according to the plans Uma drafted, so the wedding is the least of our concerns. If anything, it will be a well-laid trap to lure these culprits out into the open."

"I wish I believed you were teasing, but you really do want to use our wedding as bait, don't you?" Perry shook his head. "*That's* why you're refusing to postpone? You think our wedding will draw them out of whatever wretched hole they're hiding in."

Tightening her grip on his arm, her eyes reflected a dark, calculated sorrow. "You know me too well, my love."

Chapter Thirteen

George's armored figure barged in on them a few moments later.

"Is this what you think 'stay in the throne room' means, Duchess?" he snapped, his heated gaze darting between the couple. "Perry, her safety is of the utmost importance. She shouldn't be off gallivanting."

Jax raised her hand, giving him a silent reprimand. "I'm hardly off gallivanting, George. Last I checked, I had five guardsmen in this alcove, alone."

From the shadows of the small memorial garden, five men emerged, looking sheepish, no doubt for having witnessed the terse exchange between the Captain and their sovereign.

Rolling his shoulders, George regained his composure. "Regardless, you still would be safer in the throne room."

"Are you worried about an attack?" Perry asked.

"No, I just—" a flustered George rubbed the back of his neck. "I'm concerned, that's all. Up until conversing with an established thug, we had no idea there was a mounting rebellion against our duchy. I'm worried what other news has slipped through the cracks."

Jax placed a hand on George's forearm. "We also learned from said thug that this faction is nameless and undetected by the realm's most sophisticated criminal organization. The rebels weren't even within Saphire's borders until now," she pointed out. "How could you possibly be blaming yourself for not being aware of them?"

"Indeed," Jaquobie murmured as he joined them in the grove. "If it is anyone's failing, it is mine, Duchess. My courtiers abroad in the other duchies have uncovered nothing about this growing tension. It's as though this group is made of phantoms."

Before Jax could chastise him as well, Perry spoke up. "Given that, can we really trust that this Signor Daephanté has provided accurate information?"

"I believe his unease was genuine," Jax stated. "With the warnings he issued, we have no choice but to believe him."

"Jaquobie and I have outlined a safe way to escort our guests home with Ducal Guard, allowing us to postpone the wedding and eradicate this threat before it gets out of hand," George explained.

With a stiffening jaw, Jax said, "We are *not* postponing the ceremony."

"Your Grace," Jaquobie began. He hesitated a few seconds before continuing. "It is easier for Saphire to protect merely its own within the castle walls."

"It may be easier for Saphire for the time being, but how will it look to the other nations if the supposedly strongest duchy in the realm cowers to some phantom shadow?" Jax glared at her advisor. "I know this will make me sound heartless, but it is coming from a place of authority. I cannot justify sending the entire realm home because one member of my court has been kidnapped. The other rulers will question my ability to carry on in a crisis if we…if we bar the gates."

Jaquobie's shoulders squared. "Then what do you suggest we do?"

She thought for only a few seconds. "Fortify the castle and ensure our guests are well-protected. If anything, these rebels will target the wedding itself. Our goal is to thwart them before that happens." Jax paced around the alcove. "Every caravan arriving will be thoroughly searched from top to bottom. No one will enter without proper vetting. With these measures in place, we might be able to catch these conspirators."

"It's a dangerous gamble you're taking," George said, his expression unreadable.

She stopped her pacing to answer him. "I can't lose both Uma *and* Saphire to these brutes."

Jaquobie spoke up. "We already dispatched missives to our network of spies to see if they can unearth anything knowing what we know now, but timing is not on our side." He squinted up at the blazing sun. "Duke DeLacqua will be arriving within the hour."

"We carry on as is," Jax instructed, motioning for Perry to follow her. "We'll see to our guests and then come inside to prepare to greet the Duke."

She noticed the wary glances Jaquobie and George exchanged as she left. She knew they wouldn't fully understand her reasons for demanding the wedding continue as planned, but she didn't expect them to, nor did she need their approval. *She* was the Duchess…and she knew she had to put the good of the duchy first. Baiting these rebels into action was the only way she could hope to eradicate them *and* save Uma.

Perry's hand rested on the small of her back and she felt her tension drift away. "Perhaps we join in a game of croquette, just for a bit," he suggested, pointing to the expansive lawn as they emerged from the confines of the garden. "To help take your mind off things."

She had just opened her mouth to protest when Carriena's loud voice greeted her ears. "Well, there you are. We were beginning to think you'd gotten lost!"

She came bounding across the grass, mallets in hand. "Come on, you must help me put this caddish fool Bran in his place. Doesn't he realize *I'm* supposed to win?" Dragging Jax away from Perry's arms, Carriena raised her mallet to the sky. "Onward to victory!"

Jax laughed at her friend's wild behavior and soon got caught up in a vicious game. By the time their rivals admitted defeat, Carriena had Bran and Edmund almost in tears at her taunts.

"Where were you, love?" Carriena asked after the hooting and cheers had subsided. Everyone now sprawled out across the grass to soak up the sun. "You've been so hard to track down these past few days. I thought we all came early to spend some time together?"

Jax's cheeks ripened. "I have been a dismal hostess, haven't I?"

"I wouldn't say 'dismal'," Carriena mused. "I mean, after all, you have provided me with plenty of entertainment." Her lilac eyes drifted over to Emyr's strapping figure, his dark skin glistening in the sun.

"You have to thank Perry for that, not me," Jax said with a halfhearted laugh.

Carriena narrowed her eyes. "Is everything all right? There's not an issue of state, is there? I know I was a bit of a brat about Darian, but after having spent time with him, I do see why he's a good fit, and I'm sure Father will, too."

Jax hugged her knees to her chest. "While I am delighted to hear you've had a change of heart, that's not what has me worried."

"Ah, so there *is* something," Carriena said, propping herself up with an elbow.

Looking around at her gathered friends, Jax shook her head. "Now is not the time for me to share."

Carriena scowled. "If being Duchess means you can't be truthful to a friend, then I might as well give up my claim to the throne right now."

"As if you aren't required to keep secrets from me." Jax couldn't help but let her defenses go up.

"Father may wish it were so, but I'm an open book when it comes to my friends," Carriena countered. Jax's doubtful expression egged her on. "Go on, ask me anything."

Jax didn't like the direction this conversation was going. "There's no need, Carriena."

"Go on, now. I'll prove friendship means more than secrets of a crown." Carriena was now adamant.

"All right, then." Jax rose to the challenge. "What's the state of Isla DeLacqua's treasury?"

Carriena's cheeks paled, and Jax knew she'd hit the right mark. But to her surprise, Carriena cleared her throat, her eyes darting about before answering. "Father has run it dry. We've only been able to fund the duchy these past few months because he has taken out so many loans to pay for the imported goods our people need. But when the time comes to pay up, I think he'll have to forfeit the isles to the highest bidder." Her eyes became glassy. "Probably for the best, since I'm so rotten at keeping secrets. I wasn't meant to be a Duchess."

Jax could hardly believe what she was hearing. "Wh-what? How? Why didn't you come to me for help? I would have gladly provided the funds instead of you having to go to moneylenders."

Carriena smiled sadly. "I tried convincing Father to request aid, but he heard what you did for the Savantian vineyards and figured you had reached the limits of your charitable giving."

If Duke DeLacqua thought that financing a few vineyards would cap out her treasury, he obviously didn't know the true wealth of her duchy. Or any duchy, for that matter. "Darling, I'm so sorry." She didn't know what else to say. She was surprised that the Duke would opt to give up his duchy to pay his debts, but then again, depending on who he'd asked for financing, it could be either that or his life as payment if the lender was dirty enough. What would happen to the isles once DeLacqua forfeited his claim?

Carriena shrugged her shoulders, and Jax guessed she was trying to put on a brave face. "I may be staying on the continent indefinitely after your wedding. I'm heading to the Academy in the hopes of becoming a professor." She lay back on the grass, looking to the sky. "Considering I'll need a job and all."

Jax couldn't comprehend the idea. "Nonsense. You'll stay here. We can find something for you. I'll make up a title if I have to."

"I appreciate the support, but I think I'd actually like teaching. I enjoyed my days at the Academy immensely. I want to make sure future generations have the same experience."

Jax watched her friend for a moment, a friend who had just shared her innermost thoughts and deep secrets. "Uma's been kidnapped," she said abruptly, not able to stop the words even if she wanted to.

Carriena didn't move. She just continued to lay there in the sun. After a beat or two of silence, she popped one eye opened and looked at Jax before turning white. "Oh Virtues, you're serious." She sat up and spoke in a harsh whisper. "What in the hell happened?"

Jax's eyes watered at she retold the tale, from finding the abandoned carriage and dead soldiers, to speaking with Signor Daephanté about a growing rebellion. "I just feel like we are stuck, waiting for them to make the next move."

Carriena appeared to be speechless.

Jax waited for the barrage of questions, giving her friend time to process all she'd shared.

"What are you doing to find her?" Carriena finally asked. "I can only imagine you have some plan up your sleeve for rescuing Uma."

"For once, I am at a loss. The only piece of evidence I have is the letter left at the crime scene, and there's hardly anything to go on," Jax admitted.

"May I see it?"

Jax dug into her dress pocket and pulled out the wrinkled parchment.

Carriena examined the script, her eyes focusing in on the signet. "This crest has to *mean* something."

Jax gave her a questioning look. "I don't follow."

"People don't just pick a symbol at random. They choose it for its meaning." Carriena pointed her slender finger to the serpent wrapped around the sword. "This image means something to this group, Jax. I suggest learning more about it."

"Where is this sage wisdom coming from?" Jax sat back in wonder.

Carriena smirked. "You may recall that while at the Academy, I had an affinity for learning about the Ancient Faith, a religion which heavily relies on the significance of symbolism within its texts and art."

Jax's mouth dropped in amazement. "Wonders never cease. You may make a great professor, yet."

"In fact, why don't we go to the archives and see if we can dig up anything," her friend suggested.

Jax was just about to agree when a steward's signal caught her eye. "As much as I'd like to, it appears your father has arrived. Why don't we reconvene after dinner?"

Carriena grinned. "Have fun with Daddy-dearest. I'll be right here, enjoying the view," she said as her lustful gaze traveled to a shirtless, sunbathing Emyr.

Jax laboriously rose from the ground, longing to stay with her friends and enjoy the tranquil scenery, but alas, duty called. As she strode away from the garden, she couldn't help but marvel at the nonchalance Carriena had displayed over the very real likelihood of losing her crown and her home. How she could be so cavalier and composed about it made Jax wonder if the young woman truly was relieved to have a second chance at a normal life, unrestrained by the confines of protocol and court. It just went to show how different the two friends really were from one another. Despite its challenges, Jax couldn't see herself living any other way.

‡

As she walked back to her chambers after having greeted Duke DeLacqua and his delegation, she wondered if there was a diplomatic way she could pay off his debts and help him keep the isles running smoothly. As much as his charisma and bravado tried to blind her, Jax noticed his robes were worn and his carriage was in need of repair. *He must be in desperate straits if he's showed up looking like that,* Jax thought, not unkindly, but with genuine concern. She would need to spend some serious time after the wedding figuring out the best way to approach the DeLacqua ordeal.

"Duquessa, I'm thinking a red gown for this evening," Vita called from the wardrobe as Jax entered her rooms.

"Before I can even think of getting dressed up again, I need a bath." She moaned, throwing herself across the sofa in dramatic fashion.

"It's already waiting for you. I just need to add a few stones to heat the water up again," Vita said, poking her head out of the bedroom door.

"You're a blessing." Jax followed her into the washroom, smelling the lavender incense burning near the window.

"Enjoy," Vita said a few minutes later, leaving the Duchess to soak in the quiet with her thoughts.

They drifted back to her conversation with Carriena in the garden, not about Isla DeLacqua, but about the crest on Uma's kidnapping note. Carriena was right; it had to *mean* something. As the image floated in her mind, no longer ink, but a real serpent and sword, she became more convinced that she'd seen something like it somewhere before. Feeling that tingle of recognition within her imagination, she wondered if it had haunted her in a lost dream or something. Whatever it was, it was a very bizarre feeling, as if seeing the crest behind a heavy veil.

"Duquessa?" Vita's voice prodded her consciousness and she opened her eyes with a start.

"Goodness, I guess I feel asleep for a moment there," Jax said as she stood up in the tub, taking the warm towel from Vita's outstretched hands.

"You were mumbling in your sleep, Duquessa."

"Hopefully I didn't spill any state secrets," Jax replied with a grin, but her face fell when she caught sight of Vita's unnerved expression. "Did I say something that upset you?" She slipped into a silk robe and followed her maid to the vanity.

Vita shook her head as she began to style the Duchess's hair. "No, you just sounded so frightened. For a moment, I was worried someone had gotten in here."

"What was I saying?" Jax pressed. She'd never been known to talk in her sleep before.

"You kept crying 'the snake has come to get me, the snake has come to get me'. You sounded like a frightened child." Vita paused for a moment, shuddering at whatever memory consumed her.

Jax thought back to the serpent wrapped around the sword. Had her dream been some kind of premonition of what was to come?

Chapter Fourteen

A knock on the door interrupted Vita's final strokes of rouge across Jax's cheeks. Placing the brush down, the lady's maid hurried over to the outer chamber door and came back with Master Vyanti in tow.

"Greetings, Your Grace," he said with a bow.

"Is everything all right?" was her immediate response.

Chuckling, he dug into his robes, pulling out a small vial. "Vita sent word that you were having a disruptive sleep. I think this might calm down your mind when you retire tonight."

Wondering when her lady's maid had sent for the physician — had she really been nodding off that long? — she took the blue-green vial, placing it by her bedside. "I worry that if I take a dose of that, I'll sleep right through my wedding."

Vyanti gave her a fatherly look. "I made sure it was a diluted amount. It will help with the nightmares."

"I honestly don't even remember having one," Jax protested, her mind drawing a complete blank.

Giving her a wan smile, he turned to leave.

"Vyanti, why don't you join the feast tonight? I'm sure Charles will enjoy speaking with you more. And bring young Bastion, too. Why not show the boy a little fun?" It was for Bastion's sake that Jax extended the sudden invitation. She felt guilty for keeping the poor lad under lock and key, but it was for his own protection. "We'll continue to tell the guests that he's in charge of the fireblooms to explain his presence."

"I'm sure he'll be delighted," Vyanti said before departing.

As she arrived for dinner a little while later, Jax found a group of friends gathered outside the banquet hall. Skander, Edmund, Emyr, and Bran were deep in conversation and did not notice her until she arrived at Skander's side.

"Duchess!" Edmund nearly jumped out of his skin upon noticing her among their ranks.

All four closed their mouths with an audible snap.

"Good evening." She looked with bemusement at the four strapping men. "Did I interrupt something?"

"Nothing at all," Emyr said with silky finesse. "We were just plotting how to convince you that Perry's a dolt and you belong with one of us instead."

"Where's the sudden interest coming from, Viscount? I thought Lady Carriena had you wrapped around her finger," she teased. Yet, she watched Emyr's expression grow sad and drawn at the mention of her friend's name. Had Carriena grown tired of the young man since the afternoon? "Regardless," she said, carrying on, "poor Perry is stuck with me, I'm afraid."

Edmund gave her a fiendish grin. "You can't fault us for trying, Duchess."

The four friends resumed their murmuring the moment she moved away from them, skillfully keeping their words indistinguishable from her keen ears. What were they conspiring about?

Jax was the first to enter the dining hall this evening, relieved she didn't have to wait to be announced. Since tonight was the last night she could attend to her personal guests, she wished to greet them as they came to dinner.

Hendrie and Perry appeared not long after her, both appearing ripe with embarrassment.

"What's happened to you two?" Jax scoffed, wondering why they seemed so uncomfortable in her presence.

"Oh, just something Skander mentioned to us out in the hall…"

Perry trailed off, clearly not wanting to talk about whatever it was.

Imagining that his friends were just teasing him about his upcoming nuptials, Jax dropped the subject and turned her attention to Charles and Giovanna's arrival.

"I ran into Master Vyanti in the hall," Charles said with exuberance, "and he said he'll be joining us for dinner this evening. What a treat! I wonder if I could get the Academy to transfer the remainder of my residency to Saphire to study under his tutelage." He thoughtfully scratched his scalp through his blond hair. "I only have a few more weeks of the program left, but it would be an incredible opportunity."

"I'm sure I can put in a word with your professors, Charles," Jax said. "It would be wonderful to have you study here." Considering her fondness for his boyish charm, she knew his residency with the court physician in Isla DeLacqua would be in jeopardy if things went south for Carriena and her father. She could at least make sure Charles did not fall victim to the Duke's extravagant spending habit.

"You must be on the edge of your seat with excitement, Jacqueline," Giovanna gushed, wrapping her in a warm hug. "Only two more days!"

Jax's stomach clenched with nerves. "It's hard to believe."

"It's been so delightful being here. I hope we don't have to wait a whole year before seeing each other again," Giovanna wistfully responded.

"I shall make it a royal decree that you must visit more often," Jax said with a sly grin. A new thought bubbled to the surface of her mind. "You should convince your father to put on his next production here in Sephretta. We'll build him a glorious theater and everything."

Her friend's amber eyes lit up. "Careful, Duchess, or you might find yourself regretting such a generous offer."

"I wouldn't regret it at all!" Jax said in protest. "In fact, I don't know why I didn't think of it sooner. Why should Hestes be the theatrical capital of the realm?"

Giovanna blushed. "I'm not sure I could ever convince my father to leave behind his beloved duchy, even if you became his personal patron."

Jax looked the young woman over. "I'd actually be interested in securing another playwright. One that's more up-and-coming." She paused. "Have you ever thought about stepping out from your father's shadow?"

"Me?" Her eyes widened. "Jax, I'm just an actress. I can sing and dance, yes, but write?"

Jax's eyes darted conspiratorially to Charles before she continued. "A little birdie told me that you were responsible for more than half of the script about our high seas journey. And was that not a bona fide hit?"

Giovanna looked as if she fought the urge to smack her bigmouthed brother, who had shared this news with Jax earlier in the day. "It's a developing talent, I'll admit."

"Then I'd encourage you to think about developing it here," Jax replied, grinning with triumph as the Montivarius siblings strode to their seats, discussing the proposal.

Annette, Duke Mensina, and Darian arrived next, exchanging quick greetings before settling in their chairs.

"I'm starving," Duke Mensina grumbled. "Now I know where you get your appetite from, Jacqueline. The walls of this castle make a person's stomach growl."

Jax was still chuckling when Dukes Pettraud and Crepsta arrived.

"My wife is taking supper in her rooms tonight," Duke Crepsta said apologetically. "She just doesn't have the stamina these days to keep up with state dinners night after night."

"It's a slap in the face, growing old, I tell you," Duke Pettraud sympathized.

"No apologies necessary, Duke," Jax reassured him. "We want her well rested for the wedding. I'll make sure the chef sends a peach tart along with her dinner."

"That will delight her, Duchess," he replied, kissing her hand in reverence.

Carriena and her father arrived, arm in arm, and asked to be seated next to Darian and Annette. Heartened by the Duke's genuine interest in getting to know the new Cetachi leader, Jax summoned a steward to make the arrangements and within minutes all four were conversing in animated fashion.

The Pettraudian brood, as she had come to think of them, were the last to grace the dining hall with their rowdy presence. Perry's brothers seemed much more eager tonight to interact with his friends than they had the previous evening. She cringed a bit upon noticing Philippe's bruised eye, but he appeared to take it in good stride. He caught her staring at the purple mark and had the decency to look shamefaced.

"I deserved it," he said with a shrug before sauntering over to join his brothers.

Realizing it would be the last intimate meal before the festivities began—not that everyone at her ducal table could be called an intimate friend—Jax encouraged everyone to enjoy copious amounts of mead, conversation, and laughter. She kept watch at the head of the table, her eyes searching for anything that might help her understand the events that had transpired over the past few days.

Besides herself, the heads of five other duchies had gathered here, none of them appearing to suspect a possible threat on the horizon.

What troubled her most was that the kidnappers had been silent since spiriting Uma away. She would have expected some type of ransom letter, especially given the fact that she "had something" of theirs, according to their cryptic note. *Now, you can wait.* The words danced before her eyes. What was their end goal? What did they want?

"Everything all right?" Perry asked, taking her hand. "You've hardly touched your dessert."

Jax glanced down at her lemon cake with strawberry sorbet. "I need to make sure my wedding gown fits," she joked lamely, her stomach too roiled with worry to eat properly.

As everyone cleared out of the dining hall later in the evening, Carriena appeared at her side, looking grim.

"I know I said we should go dig through the archives, but Father has just summoned me for an important meeting," she said, wringing her hands. "I imagine it has to do with how we will be presenting ourselves tomorrow once the other duchies arrive. Might we reconvene tomorrow morning? Will you have time?"

"The rehearsal and reception won't begin until sunset, so I can make the time," Jax replied. She gave her friend a warm hug and wished her good night.

Perry waved his friends and brothers off, and Jax tried to ignore the shifty looks they sent her way. "What's going on with them? They kept sending dodgy signals to each other throughout the entire evening."

"And you didn't miss it, did you?" Perry drawled. "Your eyes were rolling around the room like a game of croquette."

She shook her head in her defense. "I was merely keeping an eye on things."

"You might want to try and act like you're having more fun if you don't want people to get suspicious that something is wrong," Perry pointedly suggested.

Her face hardened at the criticism. "Thank you for that observation."

He held his hands up. "You were the one who was so adamant about seeing this through."

"Any *more* advice?"

Looking tired, Perry ran a hand through his dark hair. "No, which is why I didn't like this idea to begin with. It's an impossible task to pretend everything is fine."

Her amethyst eyes flared. "Agreed. And it's even harder when your fiancé and his friends act all cagey any time I come near them."

Perry scoffed. "Come on, that's not true."

She was in no mood to argue any further. "Good night, Lord Pettraud," she said in dismissal, not bothering to wait for his reply as she stalked off to her rooms.

Vita was waiting for her, nightclothes in hand. "I figured you might want to retire early tonight," she offered before helping the Duchess out of her ruby red gown and jewels.

"Shall I put this in a glass for you?" Vita dangled the vial Master Vyanti had brought earlier between her fingers.

Laying her head back on her pillow, Jax didn't feel like taking the draft tonight. She had too much to think about, and she needed the silence of night to do it. "Leave it there, why don't you," she said, motioning to her bedside table. "I may take it in a while."

Vita complied and swiftly tiptoed out of the room, leaving Jax to her whirlwind of thoughts.

Fear and anxiety dominated them all, and an overwhelming sadness crashed down on her. She was supposed to be preparing for her wedding, one of the happiest days of her life, and yet here she was, feeling utterly useless and alone. Between Uma's aching absence, George's intense concern, and Perry's disapproval, she couldn't find her footing. She felt like she was on the brink of an abyss, one false move threatening to push her over into darkness.

Chapter Fifteen

She woke with a start, murky images of the serpent-sword crest fading from her nightmares. What was it about that symbol that caused her heart to race? She reached for the parchment now tucked in her nightstand and once more examined the inky drawing. Why was it beginning to feel familiar to her the more she dreamed about it?

Throwing off her silk sheets, Jax climbed out of bed, her nerves on edge. Shooting a look at the clock, she saw that it was almost one in the morning. As much as she knew she should take the sleeping draft Master Vyanti had provided, she decided against it. Feeling unsettled, she opted to go for a walk.

She changed into a simple gown, discarding her nightdress on the floor for Vita to deal with later. She placed the parchment in her pocket, and without a glance back at her inviting bed, she marched out into the dark hallway. This late at night, only a few lit torches lined the halls, casting an eerie glow all around.

A chill ran down her spine as her fingertips brushed the parchment in her dress pocket. Perhaps she would use this time to go to the archives, as she and Carriena had originally planned. Maybe she could find something that would decode the meaning of the menacing symbol.

Dashing down the stairwell from her tower, Jax moved silently through the palace, giving an awkward smile here and there to the guardsmen positioned along the hallways. She had no doubt her movements would eventually be reported back to George.

A door ahead creaked open, halting her in her tracks. "Goodness," she said as a lanky figured emerged into the dim light, "you gave me a fright!"

Charles rushed to her side, the door slamming behind him. "Sorry about that, Jax. I was just coming back from the library. Got caught up in some research. Master Vyanti mentioned the most fascinating method for blood thinning at dinner. I just had to read up on it."

Jax could still feel her heart racing from the unexpected encounter. "Of course, of course. I hope you found the information you needed. I'm actually heading to the archives myself."

"Shouldn't you be resting for your big day?" Charles asked, raising a pale eyebrow.

She breathed a longing sigh. "Isn't funny that sleep never comes when you need it most?"

"I'm sure Vyanti has something in his stores that could help with that." He shrugged. "Goodness, I feel like most of what I do for Duke DeLacqua involves some kind of sleep tonic."

Jax could imagine the Duke's floundering finances keeping him up at night. "I doubt even the strongest potion could ease my mind right now."

"Curiosity is the fickle beast, isn't it?" Charles said with a sly grin, holding open the door he had just come through. "Happy researching, Duchess."

She bade him good night, watching him disappear down the corridor, back to the wing of the castle where he and his sister were staying. She smiled, dearly hoping the Montivarius siblings would make Saphire their home one day. It would be nice to have friends around.

Resuming her trek to the archives, she nearly collided with a silent figure hurrying around a corner. "Bastion? What are you doing up at this hour?"

"Your Grace," the young man said, scrambling to bow before her, "I am so sorry. I didn't even hear you coming."

"No harm, no foul," she reassured him. "Does Vyanti know you are out here?"

"Oh yes, Your Grace. He sent me to tend to the fireblooms. I actually have been keeping an eye on them, you see. They should be ready by the evening celebration tomorrow." Bastion smiled at her. "They will be a sight, for sure."

"I look forward to seeing them," Jax said, giving his scrawny shoulder a fond pat. "Just make sure you get enough rest to allow for a full recovery."

"Master Vyanti says I'm doing loads better." He turned to show her the back of his bruised head. "See, the bump's almost gone!"

She laughed at his juvenile excitement. "I'm heartened to see you thriving under his care."

"Yeah, I hope I'll be able to leave soon. My family needs me to bring in wages back home," he said, growing reflective at the mention of his life outside the palace.

Jax felt a pang of guilt, as she did not have the heart to tell him it would not be safe for him to leave until this whole ordeal with Uma was resolved and he was no longer a target. "Why don't I have High Courtier Jaquobie send along a purse to your parents? After all, I need to pay you for caring for the fireblooms."

Bastion blushed. "You're too kind, Duchess."

"It's the least I could do, considering you were attacked all because of my silly wedding."

He bowed in return. "It has been the highest honor of my life, Your Grace."

She waved as he hurried back to Master Vyanti's infirmary with a slight skip in his step.

"Tsk tsk, such a shame you've given us no choice, Duchess, but to tell Perry you've been seeking the attentions of a younger man," a slimy voice taunted from the shadows of the hall.

Jax whirled around, coming face-to-face with not just one man, but Philippe, Kaul, and Elias. *Virtues' sake, is no one asleep in their rooms?* She gave a tight smile to the three Pettraudian brothers. "I hardly think Perry would believe a florist's apprentice could tempt me."

Philippe's bruised face made him appear all the more menacing in the moonlight that streamed in from the corridor's high windows. "Yes, I suppose you do have more business sense than that."

Her eyes narrowed, noting a sloshing bottle of wine in his fidgeting hands. "What are you gentlemen doing out so late at night?" She did not like the leering looks plastered on the brothers' faces. Down the hall, she could hear the ducal guardsmen moving closer to her.

Kaul must have seen the armored men approaching behind her, for he grabbed his eldest brother's arm and pulled him back. "Just clearing our heads, Your Grace. We had more than our fair share of mead tonight and needed to walk it off before going to bed." He sent looks of warning to the other two, who nodded their support.

Jax felt her stomach twist into knots, seeing through the blatant lie. "Might I suggest sending for a tonic from our court physician, then?" she recommended. She turned to three guards who had formed a wall behind her. "Will you please escort the Pettrauds back to their suite?" she asked, trying to keep her voice as light as she could, not wanting Philippe to sense her fear and attempt to use it to his advantage.

"No need for escorts," Elias said, holding up his hands in mock surrender. "We can see ourselves back. Good night, Your Grace." He bowed at the waist, motioning for his brothers to follow his lead.

"Make sure they actually go back to their rooms," Jax whispered under her breath to the nearest guardsman. With a salute, he took off, concealing himself in the shadows as he trailed the brothers.

"Your Grace, would you like a personal escort until you reach your destination?" one of the remaining sentries asked.

Normally, she would have told them not to be silly; she was perfectly safe in the walls of her own castle. But Philippe's cruel face haunted her. "That would be lovely, thank you," she said.

They ran into no other interruptions the rest of way, and within a few minutes, Jax pushed open the great doors to the library. The various fireplaces throughout the room had been doused and the candles had all been snuffed, leaving its contents covered in darkness. Taking a torch from the outside hallway, Jax stepped into the cavernous space and debated where to begin her search. Wishing she'd brought a cloak to combat the chill in the air, she stalked the lengthy shelves, scanning for anything that stood out to her. Grabbing a few tomes about the history of the Realm of Virtues, she began her quest in the hopes that the crest might have been used at some other point in history. She skimmed numerous pages on the rise and fall of rebellions during the first few centuries of the realm's creation, not once finding mention of a group that used a serpent-sword as their banner.

From there, she moved on to a few scrolls about the Ancient Faith, wondering if the crest had something to do with the old religion. Unfortunately, the Saphirian archives had very few resources about the Faith, and she quickly came up dry.

Her eyes grew heavy as the night wore on and piles and piles of parchment grew higher on her workstation, all to no avail. The sun was just peeking through the stained-glass windows when she found a book that excited her.

"A Collective History of Saphirian Nobility." She read the binding aloud, pulling the massive tome from its perch. The book was an extensive record of all the noble families throughout Saphire's illustrious history, likely updated by the scholars maintaining the archives. She briefly considered just waiting until they arrived for the day and asking then if any of them were familiar with the crest, but she didn't have the patience to delay any longer.

Plopping the book down, she began rifling through page after page, stopping every so often to examine the colorful symbols from each noble house that caught her eye. She never realized until now how many great families had risen to power then eventually crumbled into ruin over the centuries. Many in Saphire's history had used serpents or swords in their crests, but never both.

As she flipped past each yellowed page, her hopes of finding an answer sank further and further. Halfway through the book, she thought about giving up, when her fingers absently turned a page and the world around her faded away. Wide-eyed, she took in the image of an inky silver-scaled snake wrapping around a golden sword against a shield of bronze.

"How could I have forgotten?" she said in a faint whisper, her thoughts reeling as she read the text below.

The powerful symbol is associated with House Reinbeck, who at one time was a revered and prominent member of Duke Saphire's inner circle. However, when the last of the Reinbeck heirs was arrested attempting to kidnap Princess Jacqueline, the family fell into ruin and died off.

Placing the threatening note next to the book's page, she knew she'd found a match. The only difference in the crests was the position of the shield. In the book, the shield was upright. On the note, the shield was drawn upside down. And as her memories unlocked, she knew why she had felt like she'd seen that seal in her dreams. It tormented her nightmares as a child after she had been rescued from Reinbeck's failed kidnapping. How could she have suppressed the horrific memory for so long? She remembered the men attacking her carriage, bashing in her door, holding her mouth shut as she struggled. Oh, how she'd struggled against her captor's strong chest, her eyes locked on the threatening symbol embroidered into his tunic. The symbol before her now, of a noble house turned upside down and gone rogue.

"Duchess!" George burst into the library, his sword at the ready. "We have a problem."

She looked up from her studies, her eyes wild. "Reinbeck!" She grabbed the note and brought it to him. "I remember it all now. This is the same crest he and his men bore the day they kidnapped me. Reinbeck must be behind Uma's disappearance, but I don't know how. He's been locked away in our dungeons for over seventeen years."

The Captain of the Ducal Guard met her gaze with fervent anger. "The morning shift just reported in from relieving the night guard in the dungeons. They found all the men unconscious. Some type of drug, most likely. I'm having Vyanti look into it as we speak."

Fear thrummed through her body, and she guessed George's next words before they were out of his mouth. "Reinbeck is no longer in his cell, is he?"

The anguish in his eyes was almost too much to bear. "He's gone."

Chapter Sixteen

"Remind me the next time I go to put someone in our dungeons to just hang them instead," Jax seethed as she stormed out of the library. "It would save us all a great deal of trouble, wouldn't it?"

George marched silently behind her in worried silence.

"Are your men all right?" she asked, ashamed to have taken so long to express concern for the unconscious guardsmen.

"I hope so. I thought they were dead, they all looked so pale," he whispered, his dark eyes swimming with the memory.

"Vyanti is attending to them?"

He nodded. "Yes, I sent for him right away. Not only to nurse them back to health, but to detect what poisoned them. If we can figure that out, we might be able to find who did this before too long."

"You mean, figure out who amongst our guests is working in tandem with Reinbeck," Jax stated grimly. "Do you have any idea what time this took place?"

"The guards last shift change was at six in the evening last night. So right now, all we know is it could have happened anytime within those twelve hours."

Jax frowned, falling back to let George take the lead down to the dungeons. "That's a rather large window."

George ran a hand through his hair as they descended the dark stairwell into the belly of the castle. "That's why I'm hoping Vyanti will be able to tell us more about what drugged them. Perhaps a reaction time or something, anything to help narrow it down." He glanced back over his broad shoulder. "How did you piece together that it was Reinbeck?"

"I was researching all the noble houses throughout Saphire's history and found that House Reinbeck had a nearly identical signet to the one found on the threat. The only difference was that the shield was turn upside down. And that realization brought back a flood of memories I guess I've been suppressing since I was nine." She was ashamed she hadn't thought of it sooner.

George sensed her disappointment. "I was there that day too, remember? I guess House Reinbeck has been in disrepair for so long, it's all but been forgotten."

"Why now?" she asked, although she knew he had no answer. "He's been rotting away for nearly twenty years. Why make a move now?"

George held the door to the dungeons open for her, a swarm of voices coming from the other side. "Perhaps there was no one around willing to help him until now."

Hearing it from his lips, Jax shivered at the implication that one of her companions was behind the chaos. Stepping into the long passageway, she spied Vyanti and Jaquobie up ahead, surrounded by anxious, but alert soldiers.

"I've sent as many men that can be spared out in search for him, but I doubt we'll be able to catch a trail," George said as they walked past the vacant cells lining the hall.

"I hope you've been discreet about this?" Jax questioned. It would spell disaster for her if the visiting Dukes got wind that a prisoner had escaped from her dungeons.

"As discreet as we can be. If anyone approaches the guardsmen, they are to say they are on a training exercise," George assured.

She knew she couldn't keep Reinbeck's disappearance under wraps for very long without endangering the lives of her people and her guests, but she needed time to figure out how to best approach the situation.

She arrived at Jaquobie's side, and her High Courtier gave her a grim look. "I've been trying to figure out a way to spin this, Jacqueline. It's not looking good."

"Until we have someone to blame for this, I want it kept secret," she said with a hiss. "Perhaps the realm can forgive this massive blunder if we know the friendly face who's so skillfully betrayed us."

Jaquobie gave her a shrewd stare. "You believe a guest within the castle aided Reinbeck?"

"I'd be naïve not to consider the possibility. There's no way outside interference could have made it past the defenses George set up."

"Then how did they manage to escape the palace undetected?" Jaquobie countered.

Jax defended George and his men out of loyalty. "If the sentries thought they were letting a guest walk through the gardens, we can hardly fault them. We know it's possible to scale the walls from inside the grounds. It's been done before…" she trailed off.

Vyanti, apparently having finished examining the fourth and final victim, looked up, his expression drawn and weary. "These men were drugged with a plant called laceroot. It's not life-threatening, even in large doses, but it does have a long-lasting effect. Once ingested, the victims' memories from the past day or so are all forgotten."

Jax felt her heart plummet. "So they won't be able to tell us who drugged them when they wake?"

"No," Vyanti said with a sigh, clasping his hands in thought. "The perfect tool for a crime such as this."

"How fast-acting is it?" George asked. "Do you have any idea how long ago they consumed it?"

Vyanti leaned down once more, lifting back the eyelid of one of the fallen guards. "I'd say they're due to wake up soon with a nasty headache. That would mean they were drugged, oh, sometime around midnight. They would have been unconscious within the hour."

George folded his arms. "That means Reinbeck could have had as much as a four-hour head start on us."

"I think you should call your men back to the palace, Captain," Jax said. Her words drew surprised looks from everyone. "With that much time having passed, who knows where he could be by now? We need our resources here, keeping everyone safe."

"You intend to call off the wedding?" he asked.

"No." Her resolve was firm. "It's the only hope we have of drawing Reinbeck out of the shadows. Signor Daephanté told us this was a personal vendetta, and now I understand why. *'You have something of ours, so we took something of yours,'* remember? Reinbeck lost everything when my father threw him in the dungeons for treason. He wants revenge on my family, and there is no grander way to do it than at my wedding."

"This is dangerous, Jacqueline. We could be on the brink of war," Jaquobie warned.

"I doubt it," she replied coolly. "He cannot have many followers supporting him. He's been in a cell for nearly twenty years with no connection to the outside world. No, someone else has been masterminding this little scheme in the shadows."

"You mean, the person who drugged the guards is not a puppet but a puppet master?" George's eyebrows rose.

"If I had to guess, yes," Jax replied.

Vyanti interjected. "Laceroot is a very uncommon specimen, Your Grace. Not many people know about its memory properties."

"How would someone come across it, then?" she questioned.

He shrugged. "I learned about it during my time at the Academy whilst studying herbology and its medicinal uses for my physician's residency."

"Virtues, no." Jax gasped, raising her hand to her slack jaw. She pictured Charles Montivarius's sly grin after they ran into each other during her nighttime stroll. "Charles. Charles is a student at the Academy; he's a practicing physician. I saw him out in the halls last night." Her words tumbled out of her mouth rapidly as everything clicked into place. "It was well after midnight, too. He must have been coming from the dungeons."

George turned a steely gaze onto his men. "Find him. And bring him to the throne room."

‡

Jax sat on her gilded throne, clutching the arms with such ferocity that her knuckles turned white. She heard Charles's voice before seeing him escorted through the doors of the vast chamber. "Really, now, Captain, what's this all about?" he questioned. When he caught sight of Jax, his expression transformed from one of annoyance to confusion.

His forehead glistened with nervous sweat. "Duchess? Have I done something wrong?"

George brought him closer to the throne, stopping at the bottom of the steps leading up to her platform.

With calculated finesse, she examined Charles's lanky figure, watching him squirm as the silence dragged on and his questions went unanswered.

She finally asked, "Charles, can you please recount your movements last night?"

He readily acquiesced. "Why yes, Duchess. I returned to my rooms after dinner, only to head over to the archives for a bit of research." His cheeks reddened under the intense gazes of George, Jaquobie, and the Ducal Guard. "I came back, oh, an hour or so after midnight, ran into you, if you recall. I saw my sister's light on when I arrived back at my suite, so I popped into her room for a quick chat before going to bed."

"What time did you go to bed?" she pressed.

"I don't know. Maybe around one thirty?" He looked uncertain. "What's going on here? Has something happened?"

Jax sat back in her throne, wishing she did not have to look at her friend like he was a criminal. "Please, Charles, just answer me truthfully."

"I am, Duchess," he said in earnest. "Just ask my sister. Just ask the courtiers who've been trailing me around."

"Unfortunately, your courtiers retired to their own chambers after they escorted you back from dinner." Jax rubbed her temples. "But why don't we have Lady Giovanna speak on your behalf?"

"What am I being accused of?" Charles began to tremble before her. "Please, Your Grace. I am telling the truth."

She met his pleading gaze and saw it in his eyes. "I'm so sorry, my friend. I really am. I just cannot take the risk." She directed her next words to George. "Please, bring Lady Giovanna to me."

He returned with the young actress not five minutes later, her expression as confused as her brother's.

"Duchess, what's all this about? There we were, getting ready to go down to breakfast, and the next, Charles is practically being dragged away like a thug."

Jax ignored her outburst. "Lady Giovanna, can you please recount for us your brother's activities last night?"

"Is this some Saphirian wedding tradition?" Giovanna asked with a little giggle, obviously not yet understanding the seriousness of the situation.

Jax just gave her a tight smile and waited.

"Well..." Giovanna's eyes darted to her brother, who was seated off to the side of the room with a guard's hand on his shoulder. Turning her attention back to Jax, she continued. "Charles and I arrived at our suites after dinner. It couldn't have been any later than ten o'clock. He said he wanted to research some new method Master Vyanti talked about. He was gone for a few hours. I was up reading, engrossed in my book, when he came back. He teased me for losing track of time over a silly romance novel, then went into his own chambers for bed."

"And do you know if he left his chambers again?"

"No...I was asleep." Giovanna brightened. "But I'm sure our guardsmen would be able to tell you that. There were two men guarding our wing last night."

Jax felt a stab of foolishness. How could she have overlooked that? *Of course* the night patrols would be able to report to them who was in their rooms and when. They had been assigned for that very reason.

George cleared his throat, interrupting her floundering interrogation. "I sent for the night guards the minute Vyanti told us the attack happened around midnight. They'll be able to give us a full report once you're done here."

How did I miss that conversation? Jax's thoughts were muddled and her head throbbed. She realized her lack of sleep had caught up to her.

George came to her side and whispered in her ear. "You seemed so sure Charles was a suspect, I didn't want to get my head bitten off by questioning your decision."

I guess I deserve this for always demanding he listen to my orders despite his own better judgment, Jax thought miserably. Her embarrassment was palpable. She'd completely lost her grip on reason, too desperate to get to the bottom of this to see things clearly. Not to mention her state of sleep-deprivation after being awake all night. To Charles and Giovanna she sheepishly said, "You two must be wondering what this madness is all about…"

Taking the two into her confidence, she summarized the devious events that had taken place since Uma's disappearance, ending with Reinbeck's escape. Rubbing her temples with exhaustion, she said, "I'm so sorry, Charles. You must think me a monster to even remotely believe you could be capable of such a thing." Her amethyst eyes filled with tears at being such a callous excuse for a friend.

"A monster? No," he said, giving her forearm a tender squeeze. "All you stand accused of is being a concerned friend. I'm so sorry to hear about Uma. I do hope this Reinbeck bloke hasn't harmed her."

Jax trembled at the thought.

"Why don't I go assist Master Vyanti with the victims?" Charles offered. He excused himself, still looking a bit shaken from the entire encounter.

Jax turned to his sister, who looked rightly upset on his behalf. "Giovanna, I cannot apologize enough," she said for what felt like the hundredth time.

"It must be incredibly lonely for you, Jacqueline," the young actress replied, "to be so distrusting of everyone around you, even those who consider you a loyal friend."

Jax felt her heart collapse in her chest. "I sometimes wonder if I'd be better off alone, for all the pain I seem to cause people."

Giovanna took her hand. "Don't think like that, Duchess. You are worth the trouble for some of us."

"Then I haven't completely obliterated our friendship?" Jax asked, hope in her eyes.

"You'll have to try harder next time," Giovanna responded with a wink. "Uma is lucky to have you fighting for her."

After Giovanna had taken her leave, Jax returned to her chair and waited for the night patrolmen to assemble for questioning.

Most appeared in their night clothes, having been woken from sleep at their Captain's command to report to the throne room. Their numbers were impressive. Jax counted at least fifty guardsmen before her.

"I'm sure Captain Solomon has brought you up to speed on the evening's events," she announced to the room of sleepy-eyed sentries. She wondered if she looked as tired as they did. "We believe a guest within the castle is responsible for aiding in Reinbeck's escape and possibly orchestrating Lady Uma's disappearance. If you please, did anyone show suspicious behavior or leave their rooms at any time during the night?"

She saw a few hands raise and pointed to the guardsman closest to her.

"Your Grace, I was assigned to Sir Charles and Lady Giovanna Montivarius's chambers along with Neville, here." The young soldier pointed to his potbellied friend standing next to him. "Sir Charles left his chambers a little after ten in the evening, saying he was off to the library, and then arrived back around one thirty in the morning."

She nodded, relieved at the validation of both Giovanna and Charles's stories. "Anyone else?"

Another guard spoke up. "I was on patrol near the Viscounts' suites. Viscount Emyr left his room shortly after returning from dinner. He came back not an hour later, around eleven, and didn't leave his chambers again."

Jax's lips drew tightly together. "Did he say where he'd been?"

"No, Your Grace. I hardly think he knew I was there," the guard replied. "He seemed a bit preoccupied with his thoughts."

"I escorted the Pettrauds back to their rooms per your request, Your Grace."

Jax turned to the familiar voice from last night, recognizing one of the three guards who had helped her manage the unruly brothers. "That's right, I did run into those three out and about, as well."

A sentry spoke from the back row. "You may have led them back to their rooms, Geralt, but they didn't stay there."

"Excuse me?" Jax commanded the man to speak.

He marched forward. "The name's Kaleb, Your Grace. I was

assigned to the Pettraudian delegation's wing last night. The first time I saw the brothers last night was when they came back with Geralt, here. That was around two in the morning. They stayed in their rooms for a bit, but then left together around three thirty."

Jax's face went white. "Did they say where they were going?"

"No, ma'am. They just took off."

Her thoughts went back to her unsettling encounter with the brothers during her walk to the archives. Philippe's bruised and smirking face filled her mind, along with the sound of something sloshing against muted glass.

"Virtues, the bottle!" she exclaimed to George, who stood by her side. She clutched his arm for support. "When I ran into Perry's brothers, Philippe was holding a half-empty bottle."

"You think it was used to drug the guards?" George puzzled.

"It very well could be," she said, dread flooding through her. "Does anyone have anything else to report?"

The group shook their heads collectively. It appeared no other guests had been out of their rooms last night.

"What would you like us to do?" George looked to her for guidance, knowing that he could hardly just go off and arrest the future Duke of Pettraud and his kin.

"We need to speak to them. I can't go jumping to conclusions like I did with Charles. Thank goodness he's a dear friend and understood our concerns." Jax twisted her mouth. "I doubt Duke Pettraud and his sons would be so forgiving."

"Are you referring to *all* his sons?" George asked with hesitation.

Perry! How was she going to explain all this to him? "Jaquobie, bring Lord Pettraud here, please."

Jaquobie nodded from the shadows and went to find her fiancé.

She returned her attention to the Captain of the Ducal Guard. "George, wrangle up Perry's brothers, but do not use force. Just tell them I'm inviting them for some civil conversation."

Waving all her guardsmen away in dismissal, the room emptied like a cracked teacup, leaving Jax alone for the first time in hours.

†

"Jax?" Perry's call traveled up the length of the throne room. "Jaquobie seemed particularly out of sorts this morning. Anything the matter?"

His concern for her erased the unpleasant memory of last night's heated words. She rose from her throne and threw her arms around him. "Oh, Perry, where to begin?" She sighed, then recounted everything that had taken place since they parted ways the previous evening.

"Reinbeck escaped with inside help, meaning one or more of our guests are working against us." Jax clasped her hands tightly as she finished bringing him up to speed.

Perry's forehead wrinkled with worry. "Who would do such a thing?"

She swallowed the ball of guilt in her throat. "I just got done questioning members of the night patrol, and it appears that only a few select parties were out of their rooms last night." She paused, steeling herself for his reaction. "Sir Charles, whom I have already vetted and cleared of any wrongdoing; Viscount Emyr, who left for a short while and returned long before the crime was committed; and—" she swallowed before concluding, "…and your brothers."

"My brothers?" Perry repeated. "My *brothers*? You think my *brothers* did this?"

Jax gripped her hands so tightly her knuckles went pale. "No, of course I don't want to believe they did this, but I cannot say I have no doubts. I ran into them myself last night, on my way to the library. Philippe had a half-empty bottle in his ha—"

"A bottle that you think drugged the guards in the dungeon?" Perry interrupted.

"Jax," George called from one of the side chambers, his footsteps growing louder as he approached. "The Pettrauds are not in their suites."

Perry cringed. "Jax, it's not what you think…"

She whipped her head in his direction. "Perry, I know they're your brothers, but you can't overlook the mounting evidence that seems to be piling up against them."

"I know where they went, Jax!" he said, his voice loud with urgency and looking like he might burst. Calming himself down, he continued, "I know where they went, and I know why they were out and about the castle last night."

At a loss for words, she could only wait for him to explain.

"They came to my suite after dinner," Perry began, "doing their best to convince me to have one last hurrah with them. Some glorious brotherly celebration. A stag night, if you will," he admitted, his ears the color of a blooming rose. "Apparently, my socking Philippe somehow won their affection. They had tried to convince my friends to help arrange it, but they all bowed out. I, of course, refused the offer as well, and they decided to go off and have a night of wild abandon on my behalf."

Realization dawned on Jax, and her mouth dropped open. "Your brothers are at a *brothel*?"

"I told them to go to Lady Ophelia's," Perry responded sheepishly, referring to the well-known establishment on the outskirts of Sephretta. "You'll find them there, Captain."

Jax threw her head back and laughed at the absurdity. Now, the cautious way Skander, Edmund, Bran, and Emyr had been acting before dinner last night made sense. They had been trying to keep the Pettrauds' plans a secret from her. Tears streamed down her cheeks, and her stomach throbbed by the time she regained control of herself.

"Are you all right?" Perry was looking at her as though she was anything but.

"How the mighty have fallen," she said with a snort. "I used to be able to figure puzzles like these out, dearest. Here I was, ready to accuse your brothers of murder, kidnapping, and treason, when in fact, they're having the time of their lives at a brothel." Her laughter abruptly transformed into guilt-ridden sobs as her failure to find Uma's kidnapper crashed down upon her.

Perry gathered her in his arms, holding her close.

"What am I missing?" she pleaded through her whimpers. "Uma's life is at stake, for Virtues' sake."

He didn't have an answer for her. Perry simply tightened his embrace.

Chapter Seventeen

Unknowingly throwing salt on Jax's wounded pride, Philippe, Elias, and Kaul sauntered into the banquet hall later that morning, clearly pleased with the intimate pleasures Lady Ophelia's had provided. Jax had barely touched the apple-cinnamon cake before her, and upon seeing their smug faces, she knew her appetite would not return.

Everyone currently residing in the castle attended the late formal breakfast that morning, reveling in the remaining hours before wedding guests filled the halls. Jax fielded concerned glances from Carriena, Charles, and Giovanna throughout the whole meal, and she tried to reassure them with a smile, worried that their anxious demeanor would alert the others that something was amiss.

Jax found herself near the castle entrance a while later, pacing as she watched the gate for any new arrivals. Captain Solomon had organized a search party to secure each caravan before it was allowed entry into the palace, therefore making it slow going for her guests. She wanted to mitigate any tension that they might feel at the search by being there to personally greet them when they finally stepped out of their carriages.

Her eyes detected squads of archers positioned along the tops of the walls, keeping watch over the border in case someone decided to rush the fortress. She hoped none of her guests would notice them, for she found their presence unnerving.

The gate laboriously parted, and Jax watched with curiosity as a small wagon pulled by a donkey rolled through. *I can't imagine anyone I know arriving in that.*

The fresh-faced woman who'd been steering the cart leaped out of her seat and curtsied beside her donkey. "Your Grace! What an honor. I did not expect you to greet me what with all that is going on."

"I'm sorry, I don't believe we've met?" Jax wondered why this woman had been allowed entry.

"Virtues, no. I...I suppose we haven't. I've been dealing with Lady Uma throughout this whole affair," the woman stammered through her furious blushing.

Jax's eyes trailed to the contents of the wagon, taking in the beautiful display of Saphirian irises and emerald green orchids from Pettraud. "Oh, you must be the florist!"

"Yes, Your Grace. My name is Babette. I've come with the delivery Lady Uma requested for the centerpieces for your rehearsal reception." She motioned to the bed of flowers. "I can also check in on the fireblooms as well, just to make sure they're all set to blossom this evening."

Jax waved a hand. "Oh, you don't have to trouble yourself with the fireblooms. Your boy Bastion has been doing a fine job with them. We've been sort of taking care of him for a few days."

"Bastion?" Babette's nose wrinkled.

"The apprentice you sent along with Lady Uma to deliver the fireblooms?" Jax felt silly for having to remind to the woman about her own employee.

"I didn't send anyone with Lady Uma, Your Grace."

"Then who—" Jax lost her words as scenes of the overturned carriage replayed in her mind. Both guardsmen lay brutally slaughtered, yet Bastion had only suffered a blow to the head. A blow, Vyanti had said, that would have killed him had it been just one inch lower. Whoever hit him hadn't missed; they'd hurt him just enough for it to be convincing. "The *boy* was behind it," she cried aloud, shocking poor Babette with her erratic behavior. "Captain Solomon!" she shouted, racing down the steps of the palace.

George appeared at the gate. "What's wrong?"

She grasped both his arms for support. "*Bastion* is the one who helped Reinbeck escape!"

"Bastion?" George repeated, taking a moment to remember the name of the boy they'd rescued.

"That woman you just let in through the gates, the florist, said she didn't send anyone back with Uma. Bastion was planted at the crime scene so that we would rescue him and bring him to the palace to recover," Jax explained with rapid fire. "He's basically had the run of the castle for the past few days. I saw him last night. He told me he was checking in on the fireblooms." Jax felt foolish for overlooking the seemingly innocent boy who had played his part so well. "He was staying in the infirmary under Vyanti's watch. There wouldn't have been a guard posted in that part of the castle."

"Which is why no one reported his movements last night," George said with a growl.

"And I stupidly forgot to mention that I ran into him. Between Charles and Perry's brothers, he was just kind of…"

"Forgettable?" George finished her thought. "Exactly what he was hoping for, I'm sure."

"Ah, Jacqueline, there you are," Vyanti's voice called from the steps of the palace. "Jaquobie told me you were out here."

"Master! Just the man we needed to see," Jax exclaimed as she gathered up her skirts and ran to the man's side. "Have you seen young Bastion this morning?"

"Well, that's what I was coming to ask you. He left me a note saying that you'd given him permission to return home." The man's gray brow furrowed. "Now, I thought we intended to keep him here until Lady Uma's attackers had been brought to justice."

"He *is* one of Uma's kidnappers," Jax revealed. "He tricked us into thinking he'd been a witness to the attack." She explained how Babette's arrival triggered the final piece of the puzzle.

Vyanti looked visibly shaken at this news. "I'm afraid I have no idea where he's gone. The boy didn't speak about himself much."

Jax stamped her foot against the ground. "Well, now that they have Reinbeck, what do they need Uma for? They've gotten what they want."

The entry gate groaned open, drawing their attention to one of George's lieutenants. "Captain, there is a man at the gates claiming to have valuable information for the Duchess. He says his name is Signor Daephanté."

Jax and George shared raised eyebrows with one another.

"It could be a trap," George offered.

"It would be quite unrealistic for Signor Daephanté to come to our gates, lined with soldiers and expect to pull off some type of attack," Jax countered. "He's a smart man."

George's eyes darkened. "For a crime lord." To his man at the entrance he called, "Bring him inside the walls."

Jax spied Daephanté's signature blue and gold tunic fluttering in the breeze as he approached on foot with several escorts.

"Duchess," he greeted her, bowing at the waist.

"You're stretching the limits of your immunity, Signor," she remarked.

His lips curved into a scheming smile. "I was in the midst of following Captain Solomon's suggestion, leaving that lovely little lakeside cottage behind, when I happened upon a small encampment of men," he explained, pausing as he met Jax's curious gaze, "A group of men bearing that seal you showed me."

"Why would you tell us this?"

"I'd rather Saphire deal with these rogues than having to waste the blood of the Shadow Brethren to snuff them out," he replied with grim candor. "The guild does not tolerate competition, Duchess."

Jax gripped George's arm, hardly believing their luck. "Could you draw us a map to this location, Signor?"

Daephanté looked around at the armed men encircling them and chuckled. "I'm touched you're pretending I have a choice, Duchess. I come, of course, to offer my services."

The way the words slid off his tongue made her shiver. She might very well be making a deal with a monster, but Virtues forgive her, she was *this* close to finding Uma.

"Your help is greatly appreciated," she said in a careful reply.

Daephanté's grin widened. "A bit of parchment and a quill, please."

They had their heading not five minutes later.

"I'll take forty men with me." George folded the map and tucked it away in his armored breastplate.

"Are you sure that's enough?" Jax asked. "What if Daephanté was wrong about their numbers?" Her eyes blazed with anticipation.

"Do you think he's luring us into a trap?"

Jax looked over her shoulder, to where the curious Shadow Brethren member stood, surrounded by her guards. "It would be a death sentence for him, if that was the case. No, I believe he's telling the truth." She turned her worried gaze back at George. "But I fear that this generously given information is going to cost me dearly in the future."

"I'll take sixty men. I still want the castle at full watch, so I'd rather not pull any more from their posts, especially as guests begin to arrive." George pulled the parchment back out and examined the crudely drawn map once more. "If I'm right, there's a cliffside overlooking this part of the Syphir River's embankment. I'll take my men through here. That way, we'll be able to assess the area before engaging and make sure our numbers will be enough to end this." He hesitated, considering his next words. "Do you want us to attack to kill or capture, Your Grace?"

She realized how lucky she'd been since taking the Crown that she'd never had this type of discussion with her Captain before now. She did not relish taking lives, no matter how terrible their deeds, and the decision weighed heavily on her soul. "Capture if you can. I want to hear for myself the story behind this rebellion. We will let the public judge their crimes." She gripped his arm, forcing his attention to her ardent glare. "Whatever you do, Captain, see that Uma is brought back unharmed."

He took a step back, breaking their connection. "Your Grace, it is my duty to do everything in my power to stop this budding rebellion. My men and I will do our best to see Lady Uma back to safety." He bowed and walked away to assemble his forces. "I'm doubling your personal guard whilst I am gone," he called over his shoulder.

Jax watched him go, not entirely satisfied with his pledge. His words conveyed that protecting the Crown was his number one concern, not recovering Uma. Looking at the sun nearing its high point in the sky, she guessed it was nearing lunchtime. The rehearsal reception was hours off, and Signor Daephanté had found Reinbeck's men in the hills not an hour west of Sephretta. "Plenty of time to take a refreshing ride across the countryside," she mused aloud. Her heart yearned to rescue her lady-in-waiting, drowning out her mind's protests for sleep. If George and his men were not able to guarantee Uma's safe return, then she would not rest until she found a way to do it herself.

Her immediate obstacle was what to do about her surplus of guardsmen. They would no doubt try to stop her from leaving the castle grounds. Virtues, anyone she came across would likely try to stop her. She was getting married tomorrow, after all. "I know it's foolish for me to put myself in such danger, but I couldn't live with myself if something happened to Uma," she seethed under her breath, walking back toward the palace. She cringed upon hearing her sentries fall into step behind her. How could she get rid of them without raising the alarm?

Lost in tumultuous thoughts, she nearly walked into Charles and Giovanna as she rounded the corner of one of the long hallways.

"Good gracious, Duchess!?" Giovanna said, her hand flying to her heart, while a concerned Charles asked, "Is everything all right?"

"Any news about Lady Uma?" Giovanna inquired.

Studying the two fair-haired siblings, an idea sparked. "Yes, it's been quite the eventful morning. Why don't you two come with me?" Jax beckoned them to come with her.

They did as she requested. "Why, is this your personal wing?" Giovanna marveled shortly afterward as they entered a quieter section of the palace.

"Yes, it's been off limits to everyone for security purposes," Jax said, rolling her eyes with mock disdain.

"We're not going to be dragged to the throne room and interrogated for being here, are we?" Charles teased.

Jax's cheeks ripened, but she was grateful that he already viewed the memory a humorous one. "I suppose I deserve that, but no. If anything, you'll be bestowed a Saphirian Medal of Valor by the end of all this."

He cocked his head. "Whatever do you have in mind?"

She held a finger to her lips, titling her head slightly to indicate the twelve guardsmen marching behind them.

Only when they were in the confinements of her sitting room did she share her plan. "I need to sneak out of the castle."

"That doesn't seem very wise…" Giovanna looked to her brother with alarm.

"It most certainly is not, but I've got to do it. George has taken a battalion of men to invade Reinbeck's camp." Jax impatiently tapped her foot.

"That's not a good thing?" Charles asked.

Jax met his gaze. "He cannot guarantee that Uma won't be harmed during the attack."

Amusement crept across his features. "And you can?"

Jax silently conceded that the more she shared her plan aloud, the more ridiculous it sounded. "Well, yes, that's my intention."

"No offense, Duchess, but you're hardly equipped to defend yourself if things get out of hand," Charles said, not bothering to sugar-coat his words.

She made a face. "Then what do you suppose I do?"

"Number one, you don't have to do this alone," he countered.

"I can't just ask my guardsmen to ride out with me." Jax balled her hands into fists. "I wouldn't be surprised if George ordered them to put me in the dungeons if it came to that."

Giovanna drew in a shocked breath. "Your own guardsmen will defy your orders like that?"

"If the safety of the duchy is at risk, they will," she grudgingly explained.

"I wasn't referring to the Ducal Guard, Duchess," Charles clarified. "Giovanna and I will help in any way we can, and I'm sure there are other guests here who would be willing to do so, as well."

Jax considered his proposal. Opening the door of her chambers, she motioned to one of her guards. "Send for Lord Pettraud, Duke Cetachi, and Hendrie, please."

Ten minutes later, all three men gathered in her sitting room, winded from dropping whatever they'd been doing and rushing to her summons.

Considering Darian was completely unaware of Uma's disappearance and all that had been happening behind closed doors, she quickly had to rehash the past events and bring him up to speed. To his credit, his attention didn't waiver. She then recounted how she'd learned Bastion was not the young innocent she believed him to be, the visit from Daephanté, and George's plans to go after Reinbeck.

"So, that brings us here." Jax felt overwhelmed by it all.

"And you're concerned Captain Solomon won't be able to stop harm from coming to Uma during the attack?" A mask of worry painted Hendrie's pale face.

Jax, fighting off sleep, rubbed her temples. "His main goal is to stop this uprising. With all that's at stake, plus the visiting dignitaries and the wedding, we cannot allow this thirst for revenge against Saphire to fester. But it's a double-edged sword. Who knows if George will be able to get to Uma before Reinbeck decides to do something drastic?"

"Why can't he just sneak in and get her before the fighting starts?" Hendrie suggested.

Perry, standing by her side, came to her defense. "As much as we all care for Uma, if something went wrong while they were trying to rescue her, it could spell tragedy for Saphire. George and his men can't risk being detected before they ambush Reinbeck."

"So what do we do?" Hendrie's wild eyes went from Perry to Jax.

"*We* will be the ones to sneak in and save her," Jax explained. "I saw the map; I know where their camp is. We'll be able to watch the Ducal Guard from the cliffs, then climb down. There are bound to be a few moments of chaos once the fighting starts before Reinbeck and his men realize what's happening. That will be our window to find Uma and get her out of there."

Perry grimaced. "I don't like your use of the word *we*."

Jax couldn't resist an impish grin at how futile his protest was. "I'm going with you, whether you like it or not."

"Jax," Darian sputtered, "surely Hendrie, Charles, Perry, and I can handle this. You're the Duchess of Saphire, for Virtues' sake."

"And you're the Duke of Cetachi. I don't see anyone objecting to *you* being a part of this merry little band," Jax said, bristling at the double standard. "I can wield a blade. My father and George taught me personally."

Perry's shoulders heaved with a sigh as he placed a comforting hand on her forearm. "We're not suggesting you aren't capable of doing this, dearest. Goodness knows you are." He paused, looking around at their circle of friends. "But you must think of the greater good of the duchy."

"I am," Jax replied with cool finesse. "For, if something happens to Uma and I stood by doing nothing, I'd fall into despair and Saphire would go to ruin."

"We both know you'd never let that happen." His lavender eyes held her fiery gaze.

"All right, maybe not," she admitted, "but I'm going nevertheless. None of you are as familiar with Saphire's lands as I am, and you'll need my help to at least get you to where Uma is being held." She realized she sounded a bit childish in her refusal to yield, but didn't care.

"Fine," Perry conceded. "You'll lead us as far as the cliffs, then we'll approach the camp from there alone."

She didn't object, knowing she had to choose her battles wisely. "Fine. But we need to move now. George and his men have already had a head start. They'll be forced to proceed slowly, due to their numbers, so we might just catch them yet."

"How are we going to get you out of the castle without causing a scene with the guards?" Darian asked.

Jax cast an encouraging look at Giovanna. "Hopefully, with the help of a realm-renowned actress."

Giovanna's eyes widened. "How can I be of assistance, Duchess?"

Jax disappeared into her bedroom, emerging a moment later with two nearly identical cloaks. "Do you have any shoes that might make you a bit taller?" she asked, looking her friend up and down with a calculated eye.

"Why, yes…" Giovanna answered hesitantly.

"Excellent. If you would put those on, as well as this." She handed Giovanna a cloak. "There's an alcove in the garden that I'd like you to sneak into and just sit there," Jax plotted. "Bring that book you were reading last night to keep you busy."

"How is that going to help you get out of the castle?" Perry questioned.

"I used to scale the walls of the garden when I was a child to slip out of the palace," she explained. "I'll simply lead my guard to the alcove and tell them I'm going to spend some time reading. With Giovanna already in place as a decoy, I'll climb the ivy and be free. Any time they look in to check on me, they'll see a hooded figure, reading."

Her plan was met with blank stares.

Charles was the first to break the incredulous silence. "You're going to climb the garden wall? Won't there be guardsmen patrolling the border?"

"Well, if that's the case, you'll just have to distract them," Jax said in retort, a little put out that they were all being so slow on the uptake.

Perry smirked at her impatience. "Yes, with a plan like that, what could possibly go wrong?"

✝

"If anyone comes looking for me, please tell them I wish not to be disturbed." Jax gave each of her sentries a warning glare. "I've already informed High Courtier Jaquobie that I will receive all my guests at the start of the rehearsal reception." He hadn't approved of her instructions, of course, but it was the only way she could cover her absence for the next few hours.

Pulling up the fur-lined hood of her midnight blue cloak, she spoke loudly enough for all twelve guards to hear. "My, it is chillier than I thought it would be today. Good thing I have my furs." She gave them a flippant wave before pushing open the gate to the inner garden sanctuary.

She didn't come to this spot much anymore, even though it was meant to be a quiet haven for the Dukes and Duchesses of Saphire to reflect. Too many memories of false friends and murderous deeds lingered from days long past. But she pushed away her unease, smiling at Giovanna, who was already in place with her hood up and a book in hand. With her back to the entrance, she appeared a mirror image of Jax's figure.

"Good luck, Duchess," she whispered, keeping her voice low in case any members of the Ducal Guard were listening.

Jax gave her a quick, but fierce hug before removing her cloak and tucking it underneath the solitary stone bench. Her riding clothes were not ideal for scaling a leaf and vine-infested stone wall, but she would make do.

With a helpful boost from Giovanna, she grabbed the thick vines and pulled herself up, the muscle memory returning with vigor from the days of her youth. With much more agility than she thought she still possessed, Jax poked her head carefully over the top of the wall. Hendrie stood beneath it, the reins of Mortimer and his own steed in his hands.

"Duchess! Perry and Darian are keeping the southern scouts preoccupied and Charles is distracting the archers, but we have to go *now*," he hissed, urging her along.

"All right, all right," she muttered, quickly using the vegetation to lower herself down the other side. She let go halfway and dropped the rest of the way, hitting the ground with a graceless thud.

"Goodness! Are you all right?" Hendrie asked, helping her to her feet.

Jax brushed off her riding skirts as she regained her breath, giving him an impish smirk. "You said we needed to get moving."

They took off on horseback, riding away from the fortress, and within a few moments, Perry, Darian, and Charles caught up to them, each clad in their own steely armor, swords at the ready.

"Charles, I didn't realize a physician would be so well-equipped," she commented as she appraised his shining breastplate.

His youthful face hardened. "A nobleman is always ready to defend his house, regardless of his chosen path in life."

Taking the lead, Jax kicked Mortimer into a gallop, plunging into the forests surrounding the castle. She was careful of which paths she chose, for she did not want to run into George and his men. Worrying about her antics was the last thing the Captain of the Ducal Guard needed.

"We'll take this path to the top of the cliffs. Captain Solomon wouldn't risk his men going up this road, as it is much too narrow, but our little crew will be fine," she explained an hour later as they arrived at the base of craggy hills overlooking the Syphir River.

"Lead the way," Perry directed. She saw his grip tighten on his weapon. He was a trained knight, after all.

Coaxing Mortimer forward, she led the way up the steep path.

"Too bad we don't have time to enjoy the view," Darian said with a low whistle as he hopped off his mount, surveying the picturesque scene at the top.

Jax had to admit that the cliffs beautifully showcased the sprawling valley, but she didn't admire it for long. "Can you see the camp anywhere?" Her eyes snaked along the banks of the serene river.

"I see the Ducal Guard," Hendrie exclaimed, beckoning them over to his perch on the ledge. "Down to the east."

Jax followed the trail of his finger and spotted her banner hidden down amongst the dense trees. "They must already be approaching the rebels." She balled her fists. They were running short on time.

"I see the camp ahead of them. About twelve tents," Perry reported. "It sounds like Signor Daephanté did not lead us astray."

"I think we could make it down there fairly quickly." Darian's bronze eyes trailed over the ledge. "Might be a little tricky, but I think we can manage to scramble down."

"It looks like there might be a path ten or so feet below that ledge over there." Charles pointed to a worn stretch of dirt carved into the cliffside. "We just need to be careful we don't break any bones dropping down."

Jax looked at her escorts, worried for their safety now that she saw what they were up against. "Be careful, please."

Nodding, Perry kissed her, apparently not caring that they were in the company of others. "Hendrie," he said as he pulled back from her, "I want you to stay here with the Duchess."

"What?" Hendrie cried, clearly distressed by this request. "No, I'm coming with you!"

Perry gave him a sharp look. "I need you to stay here and…" he paused, as if searching for words that would not diminish Jax's fighting skills or her pride, "…watch her back."

Hendrie's brown eyes darkened in a scowl but he did not protest further.

"Good luck," Jax whispered as Perry, Darian, and Charles all disappeared down the steep ledge.

Her eyes danced between the Ducal Guard's stealthy approach and that of her fiancé and friends. Beside her, Hendrie fumed in the tense silence. She didn't necessarily blame him, for she, too, wanted to be there to help Uma, but she knew that foolhardiness could only go so far. Simply by being here, she had placed the entire security of Saphire at risk. The least she could do was keep a safe distance away.

"They're striking," she cried, watching the vanguard of soldiers pick up speed, their lancers aimed at the unsuspecting tents. She tried to locate Perry, Darian, and Charles through the leafy canopy, but they had slipped away from her sight. She prayed to the Virtues that Reinbeck's men would be too busy dealing with the Ducal Guard to notice Perry and company approach from the west.

Jax watched the scene unfold before her, helplessness gripping her chest. Battle cries echoed through the valley as the tents fell to the ground. She gasped in horror as one even caught fire. "Oh Virtues, please let them be all right," she pleaded aloud, her hands clawing into the earth beneath her crouching position.

"Jax! Jax, look!" Hendrie grabbed her arm, almost causing her to tumble forward down the cliffside. Unaware of the near mishap, he frantically pointed down to the base of the ledge. "He's getting away with her!"

Jax's eyes flashed to two figures scurrying away from the chaos. Even from atop the ledge, she could hear Uma's shouts of protest as Bastion dragged her away.

Chapter Eighteen

"We can't let him get away!" Jax cried, jumping to her feet and surveying the rocky ledge beneath them. "Come on, we'll head them off at the pass." Without waiting for Hendrie to reply, she threw herself onto Mortimer's saddle and dashed down the path from which they had come.

Glancing back to make sure Hendrie followed her, she veered off the worn trail, heading around the base of the ridge toward the crude path Bastion and Uma had taken.

She heard Uma's cries over the sound of her horse's pounding hoofbeats, pulling the reins to halt him in his tracks before leaping to the ground. "Hendrie, get your sword ready," she commanded in a quiet hush, gripping the hilt of her own small blade with fierce determination. She had never had to fight a real enemy before, but during her youth she'd been prepared for a moment like this.

"I'll go first, Duchess," Hendrie said.

Nodding, Jax crouched behind a tree. Hendrie did the same on the other side of the woodland trail.

"They're coming!" Jax said with a hiss, horrified to see her ragged and bruised friend bound by chains around her hands and ankles. The grip on her weapon tightened.

"Come on, you stupid twit!" Bastion roared as he yanked his prisoner along, causing her to trip and crash into the dirt.

"Please, free my legs and I will be able to move faster," Uma whimpered as she struggled to her feet.

"Think I don't know you'll try to run away the first chance you get? Not likely, sweetness," her captor growled as he tugged the chain once more. "Father needs you alive for leverage should this little ambush go south."

Father? Jax met Hendrie's confused expression with a frown.

"Please," Uma begged. "If you let me go, I'm sure the Duchess will repay your deeds."

"Right. You think she cares about little old you? She's just as heartless as her father. Did you know she's still going through with her wedding, even with you missing?" Bastion spat at the ground. "She's had no trouble moving on without you being there."

Jax's heart tightened as she saw Uma's face crumple. "Surely, the Duchess has her reasons," she replied softly.

Bastion snorted, jerking her forward. Now they stood no more than ten feet away from the trees Jax and Hendrie hid behind. "Yeah, her reason being that she doesn't give a flying fig about you, you filthy little commonblood."

"Or maybe," Jax retaliated as she emerged from the shadows of the wood, her sword held out before her, "it's because she knew you would make a mistake and hang yourself if she gave you enough rope."

She couldn't tell who was more stunned to see her standing there, Uma or Bastion.

"Jax, what in all that is good are you doing out here?" Uma cried, a mask of fear on her face.

"I'm surprised to see you so far away from home, Duchess," Bastion said, swiftly pulling out a threatening dagger from under his tunic with his free hand, "looking so alone."

Hendrie dashed out from behind his tree, rounding on Bastion so that he was pinned between the points of their swords. "Let her go, you swine and we *might* let you live."

"A valet and a Duchess think they can take down a son of the greatest noble house that ever lived?" Bastion threw his head back and laughed with demented malice.

"You're Reinbeck's son," Jax deduced, raising the tip of her sword to be level with his neck.

"The heir to House Reinbeck. Yes, what a glorious legacy you bestowed on my family and me, Duchess." He waved his dagger around, forcing her and Hendrie to take a step back.

She saw unbridled hatred churning in his dark eyes. "Reinbeck wasn't married when he was imprisoned. He had no heir."

"Yes, my common-born mother had me out of wedlock." His face flushed at the admission. "She was forced to flee after Reinbeck was apprehended for seeking to restore Saphire to its rightful glory by removing your father from the throne."

Jax's lips formed a snarl. "My father built Saphire to be the most powerful duchy in the Realm of Virtues."

"By making compromises and agreements," Bastion said with disdain. "My father wanted Saphire to grow its influence by force. This nation should not have conceded to anyone."

Jax marveled at the insanity in the young man's eyes. Not yet twenty, he was already poisoned by power and corruption. "Why did you do this?" she asked, hoping that the more he talked, the greater the likelihood that she, Uma, and Hendrie would be found by their friends. Seeing Bastion fully unhinged, she did not feel confident that she and Hendrie could overpower him on their own.

"I grew up fleeing from duchy to duchy, all because my mother was terrified Saphire would get wind I was alive and kill me in my father's name. I knew of the great home your family had robbed me of, of the comfortable lifestyle I could have had—*should* have had."

"That was your father's own doing," Jax replied. "His treacherous actions sealed your fate."

"The fate of an unborn child? Why should *I* have been punished for my father's crimes?" Bastion bellowed. "No, your family destroyed House Reinbeck. You tried to eradicate us, simply because of one rotten egg."

Jax felt tears sting her eyes. "That's not true. My family knew nothing of your existence. Why would we have persecuted a baby?"

Bastion faltered, and she understood this was not the story he'd been brought up to believe.

"Please, release Uma and we can start anew," Jax said with a shy purr, hoping to lull him into a sense of camaraderie.

But his grip on Uma's chains only tightened. "No, I will not fall for your tricks, Duchess. Back when news reached me of your father's death, I began crafting a plan to reclaim Saphire for my father. I could not allow my homeland to be run by someone as young and inexperienced as you. Saphire would no doubt crumble under your rule."

Her ego fumed, but she let him continue his rant.

"For the past two years, I've been gathering loyal supporters to my father's cause across the realm. Then, when I heard that you'd spat on tradition and appointed your little friend here to a role reserved for nobility, I knew I'd found my target." Bastion's maddening grin widened. "For you must care deeply about this girl to do what you did, and since you've kept me from my father all these years, I decided to take something precious of yours."

Jax's gaze darted to Uma, trying to silently reassure her that everything was going to be all right.

"From there, everything seemed to fall into place. I learned that the lady would be arriving in Sephretta to collect the fabled fireblooms for your wedding. I knew I could get you to welcome a stranger into your home if you believed I could help you track her down." A faraway look glazed over his face. "All I had to do was get one of my men to knock me on the head in just the right spot. You see, my mother was a healer in her village before she took up with my father, so I know plenty about head wounds."

"No doubt it was from her that you learned the effects of laceroot," Jax surmised.

"Ah, yes." Bastion puffed out his chest. "I didn't want to rack up too much of a body count, considering the Ducal Guard would soon be in service to my family, after all."

"You killed two of my guards, assaulted four more, and will be charged with orchestrating a rebellion that *my* Ducal Guard are crushing as we speak." Jax used fingers from her free hand to list his offenses. "It can hardly be said that your plan has been a success."

"It's not over yet," he snapped, raising his dagger higher.

"Yes, it is." Perry stepped from the shadows, Darian, Charles and George flanking him.

Caught off guard by their sudden appearance, Bastion whipped his head in their direction and stumbled on a tree root, his back now facing Jax. Seizing the opportunity, she adjusted her stance and smashed the hilt of her sword right into the fading lump at the base of his skull.

He crumbled to the ground right before her eyes, Uma's chains slipping away from his grasp.

"Brava, Duchess!" Darian's enthusiastic applause rang through the woods.

Her gaze went from her shaking hand to her sword and then to Perry and George's astonished expressions.

"I don't remember ever teaching you to fight like that," said the Captain of the Ducal Guard with a glib smile.

She took in the welcome sight of her friends. They all looked tired, dirty, and a bit roughed up, but otherwise intact. "Thank the Virtues you found us."

"Looks like you had things under control," Perry commented, his grin spreading across his handsome face.

She breathed a sigh of relief, taking a step back as Hendrie dashed to Uma's side to untangle her chains. She figured the young couple might appreciate some space for their long-awaited reunion.

But as soon as her arms and legs were freed, Uma flew to the Duchess, her arms nearly crushing the wind from Jax's lungs. "I knew you would find me," she happily sobbed, burying her face into her friend's shoulder.

Jax held her tightly, her own eyes welling with emotion.

‡

As they rode back to the castle with an unconscious Bastion bound and gagged, George detailed the results of their attack. "Reinbeck's son may have only amassed a small following, but they were vicious little bastards. Many of them died in the fight."

"Did we lose any of our men?" Jax braced herself for the response.

"We have a few serious injuries, but the Virtues were on our side today. I think Master Vyanti will be able to tend to their full recovery," he answered.

"What about Reinbeck himself?" Jax glanced back at Bastion, slung over the back of a soldier's horse.

"He knew it was over the moment we arrived," George said with grim finality. "He said he'd never go back to the dungeons and took off, leaving his supporters to fight the battle for him."

Jax gasped in fear. "So he's still at large?"

Perry took over. "Unfortunately for him, he ran right into Darian, Charles, and I. Or should I say, our blades."

Jax shuddered at the gruesome imagery. "So ends the Reinbeck Rebellion."

"We do need to decide what to do with Bastion here." George looked over his shoulder at the young man's figure bouncing on the back of the horse.

Jax studied him as well. No longer did he look the innocent boy she'd found by the caravan. "I know his mind was poisoned against my family from birth, but his actions are reprehensible nonetheless. I stand by my decision to have him hanged in Sephretta's city square."

George nodded at her order. "Consider it done, Duchess."

"I can't help but feel this is all my fault," Uma lamented, her arms wrapped around Hendrie as they rode next to Jax's horse.

"Not in the slightest, dear one," Jax said, rushing to dissuade her fears. "Bastion would have found a way to try and hurt me, no matter how long it took. But he sealed his doom when he chose to harm you." Jax stretched out her arm and squeezed her friend's hand.

Uma gave her a smile before her eyes narrowed in a mixture of suspicion and fear. "Was he really telling the truth about the wedding still being scheduled for tomorrow?"

Jax gave a noncommittal shrug as her friends shared knowing glances. "He might have been…"

Chapter Nineteen

Jax turned away from the mirror upon hearing the door of her chambers open, and she leaned her head around the dividers that had been set up in the sitting room to allow more space for the horde of women helping her get into her wedding dress. "Uma! You should still be resting."

Clad in a pale peach ball gown, Uma performed a graceful curtsy. "I'll sleep when all this is done. For now, I'm too excited."

"Shouldn't that be what *I'm* saying?" Jax teased as one of the six women working on her corset yanked hard at the lacing.

Uma plopped herself into one of the plush armchairs. "Considering last night was the first time in three days that I've not had to sleep with tree roots sticking in my back, I slept wonderfully."

Jax frowned, regretting her friend's ordeal. "I'm so sorry this happened to you, Uma. It's my fault for dragging you into this arena.

Her friend paused a moment before ushering out the throng of women. "I'll see to the Duchess from here, ladies, thank you."

Without protest, the wedding planners shepherded themselves out of the room, leaving the two friends alone at last.

"You are no more to blame than you said I was, Jax," Uma said, cupping her cheek.

"As much as I appreciate that, I think you're wrong, dear one." Jax hung her head as she spoke. "Reinbeck was imprisoned because he tried to kidnap me, and that crime destroyed his son's life."

"Reinbeck made that choice himself."

Jax felt her chest grow heavy. "Because of the position my father held, that I now hold. What is it about power that drives people to madness?"

Uma tied the laces of the corset in a neat bow before walking around to face Jax. "The fact that the answer alludes you shows your true goodness. All you have ever wanted is what's best for your duchy and those closest to you." She picked up the magnificent white dress that lay across the bed. "Your inability to fathom that type of evil is what makes you such a strong and just leader."

Jax blushed at the praise and felt her spirit being restored.

Taking Uma's outstretched arm for balance, she stepped into her gown, the white lace hugging her slender frame before billowing out gracefully at the waist. They opted for simple pearl earrings accompanied by a strand around her exposed neck, for her sleeves were designed to hang off her shoulders. Her most radiant diamond tiara lay nestled in her honeyed-curls, gathered in a simple but classic bun.

"You're going to take everyone's breath away," Uma marveled, her eyes nearly spilling over with tears of happiness.

"Hopefully not," Jax said in a teasing tone. "I don't want them all to faint. Then who would fawn over me?"

Uma rolled her eyes. "Ever the charmer," she managed before the friends collapsed into giggles.

‡

George's chocolate eyes brimmed with pride as Jax arrived outside the chapel doors. "I have no words," he said, clasping her hands as he looked her over. "There is no greater honor than to walk by your side today, Duchess."

She wiped away the lone tear that escaped down his tanned cheek. "I was worried you still might be mad at me for that little stunt I pulled yesterday."

"Little?" George chuckled, the sound momentarily obscuring the chorus of murmurs on the other side of the great door before them.

"I can't say it didn't age me twenty years when I ran into Perry out there and he told me *you* had led the charge." As his hand ruffled his short hair, Jax noticed a recent speckling of distinguished silver sprinkled throughout. "But I know how much your friends mean to you, and I can't stay mad at you for that."

"Thank you," she whispered, her throat tight with emotion.

"Although I think I may resume our training sessions after all this wedding hoopla has subsided." He sent a playful look her way. "If you think leaping at someone with the *hilt* of your sword is the best way to fight, then you must need a refresher course."

"Oh hush," she said, smacking him with the bouquet of white roses in her hand just as the doors before them began to part.

She supposed that as Duchess of Saphire, she should have made more of an effort to smile and acknowledge the crowds of people who had come to see her, but as she floated down the aisle, she only had eyes for Perry. The moment she saw him amidst a sea of blazing fireblooms, the glowing sunset creating an ethereal halo around his dark curls, she never knew she could be filled with such joy and happiness. With each step, she glided towards the man with whom she'd be spending the rest of her life, a man she truly and deeply loved with all her heart.

At the bottom of the dais, George kissed her cheeks and placed her hand in Perry's outstretched palm. She caught sight of a silent exchange between the two, and her smile widened so much it threatened to tear her face in half. After the deaths of her parents, she thought she was completely alone in the world, but seeing the fierce affection in both their gazes, she knew she'd always be surrounded by family.

As George backed away and took his place standing next to Uma, Jax and Perry ascended the stairs to the top of the dais, where Jaquobie presided over the brief ceremony.

He gave them a private smile before addressing the awestruck crowd that filled the room. "Today, the Virtues bless us as we lay witness to the joining of two hearts. May they look to the Virtues for guidance during their life together, always remembering to be kind, to be brave, to be intelligent, and to be humble in their love for one another."

Perry's eyes shone with mischief, and she guessed he'd thought of a self-deprecating joke about his own intelligence compared to hers. It had the same result as if he'd shared it aloud, as she struggled to keep a straight face.

"By the grace of the Virtues, I pronounce Prince Consort Percival Pettraud and Duchess Jacqueline Arienta Xavier husband and wife," Jaquobie proclaimed with his arms held toward the heavens. "You may kiss your groom, Duchess," he said, beaming with pride.

The cheers and applause that filled the vast hall faded away as Jax lost herself in Perry's embrace. At last, he was hers.

Epilogue

From the balcony overlooking the courtyard, Jax watched the bittersweet sight of the last carriage rolling through the palace gates.

"Goodness, I thought they'd never leave," Perry joked as he leaned against the railing. "It feels like we've been standing out here for hours."

"Get used to it," Jax said with a chuckle. "After all, it's your job to stand there and look pretty by my side."

Trying to dash away from him, her laughter floated across the castle grounds as he chased after her until he managed to sweep her up in his arms. "But then what happens when I become old and gray, my love?" he whispered against her ear.

She turned to him, cupping his face in her delicate hands. "You will always look like this to me."

He kissed her before resting his head on her shoulder, gazing out over the rolling hills covered in the shadows of morning. "It's going to be strange having the palace to ourselves."

She shifted on her feet. "Well, it won't be quiet for long, I can assure you that much."

To her delight, Lady Giovanna had graciously accepted her offer to oversee the design and creation of Saphire's first theater house. It was actually her father Michelangelo who persuaded her to spread her wings, after Jax convinced him this represented a once in a lifetime opportunity for his daughter. She also had agreed he could use her as the subject of his next production, but that was neither here nor there.

During the wedding celebrations, Jax had also found the time to speak frankly with Duke DeLacqua about his troubles. At first, it had not been pleasant, and he was furious to be seen as weak and incapable in her eyes, but after the a few days of serious contemplation about what course of action to take, she presented an offer that he couldn't refuse. She agreed to settle DeLacqua's debts with his creditors and provide him with enough money to live comfortably in Saphire for the rest of his life. In return, ownership of the isles would pass to her and be incorporated into the folds of Saphire. As much as it pained him to release the title of his family's ancestral home, he was wise enough to know Jax was doing what she could to keep his people and himself safe from any unscrupulous lenders.

This meant that Carriena, who would be traveling to the Academy to secure a fellowship position, would call Saphire her home and be back to visit both her father and her friend on a routine basis. While she was excited about getting the chance to live a relatively normal life, it was not without its hurdles. Once Viscount Emyr learned Carriena was losing her title, his affections had inexplicably cooled. After his friends departed a few days after the wedding with promises to visit in the future, Perry explained that Emyr was under intense pressure from his father to marry into a ducal bloodline, and to not hold the slight against him too harshly.

In light of the upheaval Isla DeLacqua was preparing to experience with all this change, Jax had reorganized the structure of her court for the time being. Jaquobie and Lysette were sailing to the isles to oversee elections of village and town premiers for the next few months, as well as a governor to supervise the region and report to her court regularly. Master Vyanti would travel to the islands as well, to ensure that the islands' healers and physicians were taught the latest advances in the realm of medicine that were practiced in Saphire. Charles Montivarius, in turn, would graduate from his residency within the upcoming weeks and be placed as Saphire's interim court physician.

"So, how does it feel to gain a husband and an entire duchy over the course of just a few days?" Perry asked, pulling her away from her daydreams.

She gazed across the rolling hills surrounding her home. "It all seems a bit surreal, doesn't it? I might be a fool to think it will all transpire smoothly, but one can only hope," she said with an optimistic sigh.

"I know you begrudgingly impressed my father with the way you swooped in and scooped up the isles for yourself. He's very proud to call you his daughter-in-law." He stroked her cheek, beaming with pride. "It says a great deal that the leaders of the realm were not threatened by your move, but respected you even more for it."

"Well, considering that only your father, Duke Mensina, and Darian have been made aware of the agreement, I'm sure there will be some resistance when it is all formally announced." She thought grimly at the possibility that the other duchies might retaliate with more force.

"It's a bridge we shall cross when the time comes." Perry's reassuring arms found their way around her once more. "Together."

She smiled, the warm glow of happiness filling her completely. "Together."

Murder is a royal affair.

Discover the Court of Mystery series on eBook, audio, & paperback.

The Court of Mystery series

The Ducal Detective
A Feast Most Foul
A Voyage of Vengeance
A Summit in Shadow
Throne of Threats
Paradise Plagued
Burdened Bloodline
Sovereign Sieged
Crown of Chaos
Harrowed Heir
Ravaged Reign
Innocence Imprisoned
Ardent Ascension
Eternal Empire

More Cozy Mysteries by Sarah

Trending Topic Mysteries
Glenmyre Whim Mysteries
Book Blogger Mysteries

www.saraheburr.com

Acknowledgments

Thank you to Bettye Underwood for her stellar editing and writing advice, as well as her enthusiasm for the Realm of Virtues.

Evan Grant deserves a hearty round of applause for his social media expertise as he has helped me create my (growing) online empire.

A special thank you to Mihail Uvarov, the designer of the original series covers. Your depictions of Jax will always hold a special place in my heart.

The *Realm of Virtues* map by Angelina Gennis

Dedication

To Evan, Alison, Rachel, and Liz

About the Author

Sarah E. Burr has been dreaming of being Nancy Drew since her small-town days in Appleton, Maine—but when corporate America didn't deliver any mysteries, she started writing her own! Now an award-winning author, Sarah pens the Book Blogger Mysteries, Court of Mystery series, and the fan-favorite Trending Topic Mysteries and Glenmyre Whim Mysteries. Her cozy crafting caper, *You Can't Candle the Truth,* was a 2022 finalist for both the NGIBA and Silver Falchion awards, while *#TagMe for Murder* was a 2024 NGIBA finalist for Best Click Lit Fiction.

A proud Sisters in Crime member, Sarah also runs BookstaBundles, a content creation service for authors. She co-hosts *It's Bookish Time TV*, a cozy web channel full of fun author interviews, and blogs for *Writers Who Kill*.

When not plotting her next whodunit, Sarah sings show tunes, plays video games with her husband, and takes long walks with her adorable pup, Eevee. Want free short stories and exclusive updates? Join her newsletter here: https://bit.ly/saraheburrbookssignup.

www.ingramcontent.com/pod-product-compliance
Lightning Source LLC
Chambersburg PA
CBHW061448150726

47987CB00001B/377